An Evil Invitation

"We do not wish to destroy you," she calls out.

"Could have fooled me," I reply.

"We wish to meet with you, make you an offer," she says. "Come out where we can speak. You know this to be true. We could have killed you in the bar if your death was all we wished."

"I will come out only after you have explained who you are," I say. "And don't threaten Seymour. He is all you have to bargain with, and I think we both know it."

"We are of an ancient tradition," she says. "Our line is mingled with yours, and with that of others. We hold all powers. This world moves toward a period of transition. The harvest must be increased. We are here as caretakers, as well as masters. If you join us in our efforts, your reward will be great."

"Could you be a little more specific?" I say.

"No. You agree to join us or not. The choice is simple."

"And if I refuse?"

"You will be destroyed. You are fast and strong, but you cannot survive against our weapons."

Books by Christopher Pike

Available from ARCHWAY Paperbacks

Christopher Pike

The Last Vampire 6
CREATURES OF FOREVER

AN ARCHWAY PAPERBACK
Published by POCKET BOOKS
New York London Toronto Sydney Tokyo Singapore

AN ARCHWAY PAPERBACK *Original*

An Archway Paperback published by
POCKET BOOKS, a division of Simon & Schuster Inc.
1230 Avenue of the Americas, New York, NY 10020

Copyright © 1996 by Christopher Pike

ISBN: 0-671-55052-7

First Archway Paperback printing September 1996

10 9 8 7 6 5 4 3 2 1

AN ARCHWAY PAPERBACK and colophon are registered trademarks of Simon & Schuster Inc.

Cover art by Phil Schramm

Printed in the U.S.A.

IL 9+

For Jambi, wherever she may be

The Last Vampire 6
CREATURES
OF FOREVER

1

I am a very powerful vampire. In the recent past several encounters have served to increase my abilities. My creator, Yaksha, allowed me to drink his blood before he perished. Yaksha, who originally made me a vampire five thousand years ago, was much stronger than I was. His final transfusion of blood heightened my strength as well as my senses, both my physical senses and supernatural ones. After that my blood was mingled, through the secret of ancient alchemy, with that of the divine child. I am not exactly sure what this child's blood did for me because I am still not sure what this child can do. Yet it did make me feel stronger, definitely more invincible. Finally, before she died, my own daughter Kalika gave me her blood in order to save me. And this last infusion has done amazing things for me. Really, I feel I have become my daughter, the irreproachable Kali avatar, and am capable of anything. The feeling is both reassuring and disturbing. With all this increase in power, I have to wonder if I have grown any wiser.

I am still up to my old tricks.

Killing for kicks, and for love.

In a sense, since vampires are considered dead by living beings, I killed my friend, Seymour Dorsten, by making him a vampire. But I only did this to prevent his certain death. I have to wonder if Lord Krishna will forgive me this—the third exception to my vow to him. I question if I am still protected by his divine grace. Actually, I wonder if Krishna has allowed me to become so powerful because he no longer intends to look after me. It would be just like him, to bestow a boon and a curse in the same act. God has a wicked sense of humor. I once met Krishna and still think about him.

At present I sit in a bar in Santa Monica with Seymour on the stool beside me. We are drinking Cokes and chatting with a young lady, but Seymour is thinking of blood and sex. I know his thoughts because, since drinking my daughter's blood, my mental radar has become incredibly sensitive. Before I could only sense emotions, now I get all the particulars. And I know that while Seymour flirts with the young lady, the guy at the end of the bar, with the swan tattoo on his left wrist and the shine on his black wing tips, is thinking of murder.

I have been watching this guy since I sat down, quietly reading his mind. He has killed twice in the last month and tonight he wants to make it number

2

three. He prefers helpless young females, who silently scream as he slowly strangles them. But even though I try to catch his eye—smiling, winking—I am not successful and that puzzles me. I mean, I am cute and helpless looking, with my long blond hair and clear blue eyes, my tight blue jeans and my expensive black leather coat. But I intend to kill this guy, oh yes, before the night is through. He will die as slowly as his victims, and I will not feel a twinge of guilt.

"So what do you do when you're not partying?" the girl asks Seymour. She is pretty in a lazy sort of way, with short red hair that has been cut to mimic that of a popular magazine model, and nervous glossy lips that need to be moving, either talking or drinking. She is currently drunk but I do not judge her. Her name is Heidi and I know to Seymour she is the second cutest thing in the world. Since becoming a vampire, he has conquered his virginity and then some. But I haven't slept with him, and I suppose that is why I'm still a goddess in his eyes. Seymour leans close to Heidi and smiles sweetly.

"I'm a vampire," he says. "Every night is a party to me."

Heidi clasps her hands together and laughs heartily. "I love vampires," she says. "Is your sister one as well?"

"No," I interrupt. "I have a day job."

"She works undercover for the LAPD," Seymour continues. "She's really good, too. Last week she caught this thief in the act and blew off the back of his head."

Heidi frowns, her lower lips twitching. "Do you carry a gun?" she asks me.

3

I sip my Coke. "No. My hands are lethal weapons." I know Seymour intends to sleep with this girl, and I don't mind. But I don't want him to use his eyes to manipulate her into bed. This is a warning I have repeatedly given him, that his vampiric will cannot be used to dominate human will in order to gain sex. To me, that is just another form of rape, and so far Seymour has obeyed my rule. Also, I have forbidden him to drink from his conquests. He lacks the skill and control to stop feeding before he kills a person. For that reason, when he has to drink blood, he does so with me beside him. But unlike Ray, Seymour is not squeamish about blood. He loves being a vampire so much so that he should have been born one.

"Do you know karate?" Heidi asks me.

"She is a walking Kung Fu machine," Seymour gushes.

I stand and cast Seymour a hard look. "I am going to go talk to this guy at the end of the bar. I'll meet up with you later. OK?"

Seymour understands that I intend to kill this guy. He is not squeamish about blood, but death still disturbs him. We have never actually killed any of his meals. He pales slightly and lifts his glass.

"Let me know what you're up to," he says.

"Good luck," Heidi exclaims as I step past.

"Thank you," I say.

The guy at the bar notices my approach and makes room for me. Sliding onto the chair beside him, I bat my long lashes and smile innocently. I am sweet, the type I hope he enjoys.

"Hello," I say.

"Good evening," he replies. He is terribly good

looking, and young, twenty-two at most, with a Rolex on his wrist to cover his tattoo and a seductive smirk on his adorable face. His hair is longish, brown and curly. "What's your name?" he asks.

"Alisa," I say, not being too secretive because I know he won't live long enough to repeat it. "You?"

"Dan. What're you drinking?"

"Coke. I'm on a diet."

He snorts. "What kind of diet is that?"

I laugh softly. "An all-sugar diet. Do you come here often?"

He sips his scotch. "No. To tell you the truth, this place bugs me."

I'm already tired of making conversation. I just want to kill him and be done with it. Since inheriting Kalika's psychic abilities, I have gone out of my way to kill a few bad apples. Of course, I have no intention of making it my life's work.

"Do you want to leave?" I ask.

He acts surprised. "Who are you?" he asks, with an edge to his voice.

I catch his eyes. I have a very strong stare. Just by looking at metal, I can make it turn to liquid. I pitch my voice so there is no way he can refuse my invitation.

"Just a girl. You're looking for a girl, aren't you?"

He finishes his drink and stands. "Let's go," he barks.

Out on the street, he walks fast toward a car he never seems to find. I have to adopt a brisk pace to keep up with him. People move past us in the dark, the nameless faces of a humanity I have known forever. The summer air is warm.

"I have a car if you can't find yours," I finally offer.

He shrugs. "I just thought we'd take a walk first, get to know each other."

"Fine. What do you do for a living?"

"I'm a plumber. What do you do?"

"I'm an artist."

He is amused. "Oh, yeah? Do you paint?"

"I sculpt. Statues."

He gives a wolfish grin. "Nudes?"

"Sometimes." It's so nice to get to know each other.

Yet there's something wrong, more than the obvious. He's not at ease with me, and his discomfort goes beyond his thoughts of wanting to murder me. He fantasizes how my bright blue eyes will dim as my brain dies beneath his grip. Yet I am more than just another victim to him.

He is afraid of me.

Someone has told him something about me.

But who that someone is, I don't know. My concentration is divided between Seymour and my situation. Yet I don't know why I should worry about Seymour. Certainly Heidi is not going to harm him. I scanned the girl's mind for a few seconds when I met her and there was nothing in there but thoughts of drink and sex. No, I tell myself, Dan is all that matters. I wonder where he's leading me, who we'll meet on the other end. He makes a sharp left into a dark alleyway. Naturally, to my eyes, everything in the alley is perfectly clear.

"Where are we going?" I ask.

"My place," he says.

"Can you walk to your place from here?"

"Yeah." He pauses and studies me out of the corner of his eye. Although he's striving to act cool, his breathing is rapid, his heart pounds. He definitely knows I am more than I seem, more dangerous than a cop with a gun. But he doesn't know I'm a vampire. There are no images in his mind of my drinking his blood. But the farther we walk, the more difficult his thoughts are to penetrate—another mystery. Yet I know he is worried what will happen with me in connection with another, how our meeting will go. This *other*, I sense, is also dangerous, in the same way he thinks I am.

The other is close. Waiting.

Are we going to meet another vampire?

There should be no other vampires, other than Seymour and myself.

I smile. "Do you live alone?"

"Yeah," he says, and his hands brush against his coat pocket. I realize he has a weapon there, and wonder why I didn't spot it before. The gun must be unusually small, I think. But when I sniff with my nose, I detect not even a trace of lead or gunpowder in the air, and I can smell a bullet from a quarter of a mile away. My questions pile one on top of the other, but I am far from ready to walk away from the encounter. There is a puzzle here—I must solve it.

"I live with my brother," I say.

"The guy back at the bar?"

"Yeah."

"He doesn't look like your brother." There is a bite to his remark. For some reason, Seymour is still very much on this guy's mind. Why?

"We had different fathers," I say, and my own hand brushes against the knife I wear in my belt beneath my black leather coat. Nowadays, I can kill a man at better than a mile with my trusty blade. Even good old

Eddie Fender, a psychopath if ever there was one, would be useless against my new and improved reflexes.

Dan snorts. "I never knew my father."

That is one truth in a string of lies.

There is a warehouse at the end of the block, a shabby affair built to house dirty equipment and sweaty workers. Using a key, he opens the door and we go inside. The warehouse is chock full of shelves of metal gear, the nuts and bolts of larger pieces of machinery. There is a pronounced smell of diesel fuel. The yellow lights, coated in grime, are few and far away. The shadows seem to shift as Dan turns toward me. If he reaches for his weapon, I will put a foot in his heart. Already, I think, I should kill him. Yet I want to know why he has brought me to this place, who the other is. Even though I reach out with my mind, I sense no one else in the building. He studies me in the poor light.

"Are you really an artist?" he asks. His curiosity is genuine, as is his continuing fear. He wants the other to arrive soon, so he can return to the streets.

"No," I say. "I lied."

My remark unsettles him. He thinks about his weapon—the small something in his coat pocket. He shifts uneasily.

"What are you then?" he asks.

"A vampire," I say.

He smiles, a lopsided affair. "No shit."

"Yeah. It's true." Still staring at him, I begin to move around him. He feels my eyes—I let the fire enter them, sparks of pressure. Sweat appears on his forehead and I continue. "I am a five-thousand-year-old vampire. And you are a murderer."

His upper lip twists. "What are you talking about?"

"You, Dan, your private occupation. Because I'm a vampire, I can read your mind. I know about the two girls you killed, how you strangled them and then ate a big red steak afterward. Killing makes you hungry—that's one of the reasons you do it. That's opposite of me. I kill to satisfy my hunger." I reach out and finger the sleeve of his shirt. "I'm thinking of killing you."

He brushes my hand away. Yet he doesn't go for his gun. Someone has warned him that could be fatal. "You're insane," he says angrily.

I laugh softly. "You don't mean that, Dan. Someone told you I was different so you're not completely surprised by what I say. I want to know about that someone. If you tell me now, tell me everything you know, I might let you live." Once more I reach out. This time I touch his left ear, but before he can swat my hand away, I pinch it. Rather hard, I think. He is in pain. "Talk," I say softly.

"Stop," he pleads, as I force him to bend over.

"Just a slight tug of my hand," I say, "and your ear will separate from your head. I am very strong. So talk to me, while you still can. Who is to meet me here?"

"I don't know." He squeals as I twist his ear. "I don't know!"

"Tell me what you do know."

He gasps for air. "She is just someone I know. She came to me after I killed the first girl. She said I could work for her. She gave me money. Please, you're hurting me. Let me go!"

I shake him hard. "What is so special about her? Why didn't you just kill her and take her money?"

Red appears on the left side of his head. His ear is

coming loose. He tries to straighten up and I force him back down.

"Her eyes," he cries. "She has strange eyes."

I pause, and then let him go. He is bleeding badly now.

"What is strange about her eyes?" I ask quietly.

He holds his hand to his ear, panting. "They're like yours," he says bitterly.

"Is she a vampire?" I ask.

He shakes his aching head. "I don't know what she is." He takes his hand away; it is soaked in blood. "Oh God."

I frown. "Does she have exceptional strength?"

The blood continues to drip from his ear onto his blue shirt. "I don't know. She never hurt me like you just did."

"When is she coming here?" I demand.

"She should be here now."

There is a sound off to my right, deeper in the warehouse. As I whirl to confront it, I also reach into Dan's coat pocket and remove his weapon. It is not something I can use to protect myself, not without study. It is a small rectangle of metal, with buttons on the side. Really, it looks like some sci-fi creation to defeat alien monsters.

Two figures move in the shadows beyond the towers of drawers. One is Heidi, the other Seymour. Heidi has one of these funny little boxes in her right hand, pressed to Seymour's neck. She stands behind him, using him as a shield. She is no longer drunk. When she speaks, her voice resonates with power and authority

"Throw down the matrix or I will kill your friend," she says. "Do so now "

The matrix will take me several minutes to master and is of no use to me right then so I throw it down. Heidi takes a step closer, bringing Seymour with her. It is clear, from her body language, that she is stronger than my vampiric friend. The big question is, am I stronger and quicker than she is? Seymour stands relatively still, knowing the danger is real. Heidi's expression is harder to decipher. There is an emptiness to it, an almost total lack of humanity. I wonder at the transformation in her, and realize that Seymour and I have been set up. Dan fidgets on my left, anxious to be gone. His left ear continues to bleed freely. He speaks to Heidi.

"I have done everything you asked," he says.

She nods. "You may leave."

Dan turns toward the door we entered.

"Wait," I say in a simple yet powerful tone.

Dan pauses in midstride and glances over at me, sweating, bleeding, shaking. But my attention is on Heidi, or on the creature inside her. Right then she reminds me of James Seter, Ory of ancient Egypt, the Setian that possessed Dr. Seter's adopted son. Yet there is something different about her as well.

"I don't want Dan to leave," I add softly, planting the idea deep inside Dan's mind, so he has no choice but to stay. But I am not the only one in the room with subtle powers.

"Leave now," Heidi tells Dan.

His paralysis breaks. He takes another step toward the door.

I reach out and grab him, and now Dan is my shield. My fingers are around his neck and I push him toward Heidi and Seymour.

"Release Seymour or I will kill him," I say.

In response Heidi levels her matrix in our direction and pushes a button on the side of the black box. There is a flash of red light, and I let go of Dan and dive to the side, behind a tower of drawers. The weird light hits Dan and he is vaporized. Just like that, on a gust of burning air, he vanishes on the tail of a piercing scream.

Wow, I think. Heidi has a ray gun.

In a flash, I move through the building, using the equipment and machinery as camouflage. Heidi seems able to follow my movements, but not well. I estimate her powers to be equal to mine before Yaksha, the child, and Kalika restyled my nervous system. Yet her psychic control must be greater. In the bar she knew who I was, but I knew nothing about her.

I end up in a dark corner, up high, behind a bunch of boxes. For the moment, Heidi seems to have lost me. But I know if I speak to her, she will find me. Yet I am capable of projecting my voice, making it bounce off inanimate objects. Perhaps I can fool her yet. I do want to talk to her. She continues to keep Seymour close.

Heidi finally stops searching for me.

"We do not wish to destroy you," she calls out.

"Could have fooled me," I reply.

"We wish to meet with you, make you an offer," she says. "Come out where we can speak. You know this to be true. We could have killed you in the bar if your death was all we wished."

"I will come out only after you have explained who you are," I say. "And don't threaten Seymour. He is all you have to bargain with, and I think we both know it."

"We are of an ancient tradition," she says. "Our

line is mingled with yours, and with that of others. We hold all powers. This world moves toward a period of transition. The harvest must be increased. We are here as caretakers, as well as masters. If you join us in our efforts, your reward will be great."

"Could you be a little more specific?" I say.

"No. You agree to join us or not. The choice is simple."

"And if I refuse?"

"You will be destroyed. You are fast and strong, but you cannot survive against our weapons."

"But I must have something you don't have," I say. "Or else you would not be interested in my assistance. What is this thing?"

"That is not to be discussed at this time."

"But I want to discuss it."

Seymour cries out in pain.

"This one is dear to you," Heidi says. "And you are wrong. We have more to bargain with than his physical shell. At the moment I am twisting off his arm. If you do not come out of hiding, he will be destroyed."

I hear no bluff in her voice.

"Very well," I say. "But if I show myself, you must give me your word that neither Seymour or myself will be destroyed."

"I give you my word," she says flatly.

I wish I still had the matrix with me, even if I don't know how to use it. But it is still in her sight lines: I cannot get to it. All I have is my knife. Just before I step into the light, I position it on a shelf near the circular area where Heidi holds Seymour captive. I point the tip of the blade toward them, then I appear around a tower of shelves. Heidi is not surprised. She continues to press the matrix into Seymour's neck.

"Release him now," I say.

"Not yet," she says. "Not until you join us."

"Don't be foolish," I say. "I cannot join a group I know nothing about. Where are your people from?"

"Here, and elsewhere."

"Are you from another world?"

"Yes and no."

"Are you human?"

"Partly."

"How many are in your group?"

"The number cannot be measured by human or vampire standards."

"So you know I am a vampire. Who told you?"

"You did."

"No. When?"

"Long ago." Heidi shakes Seymour and I hear the bones in his spine crack. "Enough of these questions. You join us now or you will be destroyed."

"What do I have to do to join you?" I ask.

"You must swear an oath, and offer us a large portion of your blood."

"What do I get in return?"

"I have told you. Power."

"Power to do what?"

She sharpens her tone. "Enough! What is your decision?"

Since she has a weapon at my friend's throat, I feel I have no choice. "I will join you," I say. "On the condition you release Seymour."

"Agreed." She pushes Seymour forward so that he stands midway between us.

"Seymour," I say quickly. "Leave this place."

He has been hurt and frightened, but he is no coward.

"Will you be all right?" he asks. He does not want to leave.

"Yes," I say firmly. "You cannot help me by remaining. Leave."

He turns toward the door.

"No," Heidi says. Seymour stops—there is strength in her tone. "He is not to leave. He is to be your sacrifice."

"We have an agreement," I say bitterly. "He is to be let go."

"No," Heidi repeats, and there is cold evil in her voice. "I agreed only to release him. I have done so. But to join us you must sacrifice him. It is part of your initiation."

My tone is scornful. "Is this the way of your people? You splice words so thinly they become lies."

Heidi points the matrix at Seymour's back. "Your choice remains the same. You have five seconds to make it."

I imagine she is good at keeping time. Seymour's face is ashen. He believes, either way, that he is a goner. But I have not lived five thousand years to be so easily tricked. Clearly this creature knows a great deal about me, but not everything. Since the recent infusion of Kalika's blood into my system, I have the ability to move things with my mind, as well as read minds. I have no doubt my daughter could effortlessly affect objects from immense distances. This psychokinesis, however, requires great concentration on my part and I have never used it under adverse conditions. Up at Lake Tahoe, where my friend Paula lives with the divine child, I have only practiced pushing rocks and sticks from place to place.

But now I must move a knife.

Push it through Heidi's throat.

The blade is above and behind her. I can see it; she cannot. Yet I am afraid to focus completely on it, afraid Heidi will guess what I am up to. Instead I must continue to stare at Heidi, while I think of the knife, only of the knife. Rising up on its own, flying through the air, digging deep into her soft flesh, slicing open her veins, ripping to pieces her nerves. Yes, I tell myself, the knife will fly. It can fly. The very magnetism of my mind commands it to do so now. At this very moment.

"You have two seconds," Heidi says.

"You have only one," I whisper as I feel my thoughts snatch hold of the cold alloy, a special blend of metals, far more powerful than steel, an edge far sharper than that of a razor. For me, it is almost as if I hold the blade in my fingers. There is pleasure for me in this killing. But for her, there is only surprise.

The blade swishes through the air.

Heidi hears it, turns, but too late.

The knife sinks into the side of her neck and suddenly her blood is pouring onto the dirty floor. Yet I do not take this to mean my victory is complete. Heidi's will is strong; she will not die easily. Even as her left hand rises up to remove the blade, her right hand brings up the matrix and aims it at both Seymour and me. We are standing in a straight line in front of her. I anticipate this move, and already am flying toward my friend. I hit him in the knees just as a flash of red light stabs the air where he was standing. Together Seymour and I roll on the floor. But I am quickly up and kick the matrix from Heidi's hand before she can get off another shot. My knife in her neck has slowed her down some, but she almost has it out, and perhaps she is capable of healing even fatal wounds, as I can. But I will not give her the chance. Before she can totally remove the knife, I reach out and grab her head and twist it all the way around, breaking every bone in her neck. She sags lifeless in my arms, dead, but still I am not finished with her. Ripping off her head, I throw it into the far corner. Now there is no way she can recover.

"Nice," Seymour says behind me.

"Get those two weapons," I say as I drop to my knees and examine Heidi's headless corpse. "We are leaving here in a few seconds. Her partners must be nearby."

"Understood."

While Seymour goes off to collect the two ray guns, I rifle through Heidi's clothes, coming up with a wallet and a passport. These I will study later. Feeling her from neck to foot, I find nothing else on her person. Seymour is quick on his feet. Already he stands behind me with the matrixes in his hand.

"Who was she?" he asks.

"I haven't the slightest idea." I stand. "Let's get out of here."

2

The following morning I sit beside Paula Ramirez on the edge of Emerald Bay in the area of Lake Tahoe. The sun is brilliant in a clear cerulean sky. Inside Paula's house, Seymour sleeps, a young vampire still allergic to the sun. Now the sun doesn't affect me in the slightest, and again I must credit this to my daughter's blood. Even the burning Surya, the sun god, could not intimidate the Dark Mother, Kali. Kalika's ashes rest in a vase that sits beside me in the sand. I have brought the vase with me from the house. I don't know why. Except I still miss her so, my beautiful, mysterious daughter, killed by a Setian.

Paula holds her three-month-old son, John, and listens as I describe what happened in Los Angeles. I have driven all night to reach Paula. The infant kicks his bare feet in the cold water. He looks and sounds happy. I am happy just to see him. He always has that effect on me. It was this child's blood that brought Seymour back from the dead. Yet I did not take John's blood—once I had saved him from the Setians—to save my daughter. I knew it was not what she wanted. But I ask myself over and over how I could not have wanted it.

Unfathomable Kalika, Kali Ma, where are you now?

I finish my tale and Paula sits quietly staring at me with her warm eyes.

"She said she saw you before," she finally says. "Do you think she was lying?"

"It was impossible for me to tell if she was telling the truth or not," I explain. "She seemed to operate under a psychic shield. It was very strong—even I could not penetrate it. Certainly I could not bend her will to mine."

"But there wouldn't be any reason for her to lie about such a detail."

"Perhaps. But still, I don't remember her."

Paula stares out over the sparkling water at the small island in the center of the bay where Kalika met her end. "You know I have begun to remember many things, Sita," she says softly.

I nod. I've suspected for a while that certain memories were returning to her, but I have waited until she felt ready to talk about them.

"Suzama?" I say.

"Yes. I remember Suzama."

I suspected this, but still the statement is stunning to me. Paula remembers Suzama, my mentor from my time in ancient Egypt, because she is the reincarnation of Suzama. It is the only logical explanation, and I ask her to confirm the truth for me. Paula shakes her head.

"We may be the same from life to life," she says. "But we are also different. Do not expect Suzama to answer when you speak to me. Her time was long ago."

I probe deep into Paula's brown eyes and feel a rush of joy, and of sorrow. "But she is in you," I protest. "A part of me must have known that from the beginning. When I met you at the bookstore, I knew I could not leave you. You are Suzama, the great oracle. Can't you just admit it?"

She is flattered by my praise, and yet unmoved as well. "Perhaps I can't because I'm not able to see what happens next." She pauses. "Yet I knew, when you were down in Los Angeles, that you would confront something very old."

I lower my voice. "Then you know who she was?"

She shakes her head. "I have a feel for her, that is all." Reaching down, she touches the clear water, then feels John's feet to see if they are getting cold. She adds in a serious voice. "Interesting how she mentioned the harvest."

"Yes. I didn't understand that. What harvest was she talking about?"

Paula is thoughtful, her eyes focused far away, as Suzama often was.

"There is a time coming soon," she says, "when everything will change. I have seen this in what people call visions, but which aren't visions at all. People will either move forward or else repeat what they have already done.

I have to think about this.

Suzama never made casual prophecies.

"What will people move forward to?" I ask.

"An entirely different type of life. One we cannot even imagine as we sit here. Those who do go forward will live in light and bliss."

"But Heidi was wicked. Why would she want to increase such a harvest?"

Paula wipes the water off John's feet and warms them in her lap. "There are two kinds of harvests," she says. "There are two kinds of people. Those who serve others and those who serve themselves. You know this—it is nothing new. Of course, no one is one hundred percent one way or the other. No one is a perfect sinner or a perfect saint. But where there is a dominance of self-interest, a negative harvest will come about for that person. Where there is a dominance of love, a positive harvest will happen."

"You know these things for fact?"

"Yes."

"Suzama . . ." I begin.

She smiles. "Paula. Please?"

"Paula. When will the harvest occur?"

"The date is not set. But some time in the next twenty-five years the change will occur."

"Will everyone be harvested?"

"Not at all."

"What is the criteria?"

"I knew you would ask that. The criteria, I believe, is the same for both sides, positive and negative. Yet it has nothing to do with religious persuasion, higher learning, physical health or beauty, relative importance in society. None of these qualities will matter."

"Then what will the criteria be?" I repeat.

"It is difficult to describe."

I am frustrated. "Try."

Paula laughs, and so does her child. John is for the most part a happy baby, but he can cry in the middle of the night with the best of them. Many times I have changed his diapers to allow Paula to sleep. Since drinking my daughter's blood, I seldom need to rest.

"Life is the criteria," she says finally. "Who is alive, who is not. Remember, those who are negative can be more full of life than the most positive of people." She punches me in the arm. "Take you for example."

I am her naive student, from long ago, and her remark wounds. It strikes me then how much our relationship has changed since we met. Then I was the sole knower of profound secrets. Now I truly feel I am her student and study at her knee. Mystery surrounds her like a halo. I love her so much, but she scares me.

"Am I only fit for the negative side?" I ask quietly.

She laughs more. "Silly vampire. No, don't be ridiculous. Who more than you is ready to give her life for others?"

I gesture helplessly. "But I have killed so many over the years."

She is compassionate. "It doesn't matter, Sita. Really, I know this for a fact."

I have to smile. "I suppose you would since you have such a special child."

"You understand what I am saying. The issue of harvest is separate from the type of harvest. Whether a person will go forward is dependent on his or her life vibration. Whether he or she will enter a positive realm or a negative one depends on the quality of his or her heart."

"Tell me more about this next realm?"

"I cannot."

"But you see it?"

"Yes. But words do not describe it. The next dimension is even beyond the realms souls encounter when they die." She pauses to run her hand through John's silky brown hair. How will the world react, I wonder, to a brown messiah? Of course, no race would satisfy everyone. Paula adds, "The coming harvest will affect heaven and earth."

"Is that why John was born? To increase the positive harvest?"

"Yes. But . . ." She does not finish.

"What?"

Paula frowns and then sighs. "Something is wrong. The plan is off."

"What are you talking about? What plan?"

"God's plan."

"He makes plans? Are you sure about that? I always thought he just rolled the dice when it came to us."

Paula smiles again, but the expression is short-lived. She continues in a serious tone, hugging her baby to her chest. John yawns and closes his eyes, ready for a nap.

"Every individual affects the world, but it is difficult for so many to go forward, the way we would wish them to, when there is so much evil in the world." She pauses. "Yet this evil is there for a reason. It plays its part. You remember Ory?"

"Yes. How could I forget? I just killed him last month. Why do you ask?"

But Paula is evasive, as Suzama often was. "He played his part" is all she says.

"Paula," I say. "I described to you what happened

to me that night in the desert, when I confronted Ory. It seemed as if for a time I was not physical, that the very matter of my body had changed into light. Is that related to this harvest you describe?"

"Yes."

"But when I changed, it seemed that I entered a spaceship from another world. But it wasn't a spaceship. I don't think anyone could see it but me, in my changed condition. There were beings aboard. Beings like demons, and I entered the mind of one. At least I think I did. But as time goes by, I begin to doubt that any of this happened, that I didn't just dream it all. Does that make sense?"

Paula nods. "That is why I can't describe what is to come next. It would just be a dream to us, the way we are now."

"But were these beings from a negative harvest?"

She touches my knee. "Sita. You want to understand everything with your head. You ask me to describe what you call my visions with words. But neither thing is possible. Even your brilliant mind cannot reach beyond concepts. Even your vampire eyes cannot see beyond this world. I don't know who they were, these friends of Ory. I don't know who this Heidi was. I only know that she did not lie to you when she said she met you long ago." Paula pauses and she raises her eyes to the water, to Lake Tahoe beyond the sheltered bay. "And that it was long ago things went wrong."

"Went wrong? For whom?"

"For all of us."

"I don't understand," I complain.

"Did Suzama ever just explain things to you?"

"Sometimes."

"No. She would take a lesson only so far because she was not omniscient. She saw a portion of the mind of God, but no mortal can see all of it. Suzama was not infallible."

"Is John?"

The boy sleeps soundly. Paula speaks with love. "John's a baby."

"But who was he in the past?"

Paula pauses. "I don't know."

"Suzama said this child would be the same as the others: Jesus; Shankara, Krishna. She wrote that—I saw her words with my own eyes."

"Then why are you asking me?"

"To know if it's true."

"Ah. That is the question, isn't it? What is true? But didn't Suzama also write that faith is stronger than stone?"

"But I ask you these things so I will know what to have faith in."

"Have faith in yourself, Sita. These strangers have come for you for a purpose. It does not sound as if they have the welfare of mankind at heart. You must seek them out, learn what they want and how they hope to accomplish it."

"You have seen this in a vision?"

Paula turns her head away. "I have seen too many things."

I have to wonder if she has seen my death.

"You can tell me," I say carefully.

"No."

"I am not afraid to hear what is to be."

Paula lowers her head. A tear runs over her cheek.

"I am afraid," she whispers.

"Suzama," I say, and stop myself. But Paula is already looking at me and shaking her head.

"I didn't call you as I promised I would after I fled from Kalika," she says. "Do you know why?"

"I meant to ask you. I assume you had a vision that it would be better to keep your distance. At least for a time."

"No. I didn't talk to you because I began to understand your destiny—destiny itself. It can only be lived, it cannot be explained. It is like a mystery, which ceases to exist the moment you explain it. The same with a magic trick. When you are told how it works, it loses all its charm."

"What you're saying is that you'll tell me no more of what you've seen?"

"I have seen no more, and for that I am glad."

"You look more sad than happy."

Paula smiles sadly. "Because I know you'll be going away soon."

I thought the same thing. I am anxious to return to Los Angeles to trace Heidi's background. "But I will keep in touch," I say. "I will see you soon."

Paula doesn't say anything more. She glances at the vase containing Kalika's ashes.

"Why did you bring that here?" she asks.

"To put the ashes in the water."

She nods. "It is time to move on."

Sorrow washes over me. "I still think of her all the time."

"She lived the life she was born to live." She pauses. "I never told you what she said to me when she burst into my house and grabbed hold of John. She said, 'Hello, Paula. I have no friends but I am a friend of your son's. Tonight everything will come together in a wave of blood. But don't worry, he is stronger than this night.'"

Now I am close to tears. "Her life was so short."

Paula comforts me, rubs my arm. "She couldn't stay too long. She was a star that burned too bright. The strength of her soul would have made us all go blind." Paula gestures to the vase and stands, John still asleep in her arms. "Say your goodbyes. I will wait for you at the house."

I ask weakly. "To say goodbye?"

"Yes."

My voice cracks with emotion. I need her to understand why. "I loved Suzama. I loved her with all my heart. When she died, I almost died."

Her voice is soothing. "You were younger then. You are stronger now."

I look up at her. "Will I see you again? After today?"

Suzama stares at me for a long time. It is Suzama, yes, and she stares with the eyes of humanity's greatest clairvoyant. Her eyes are dry now; she has no tears, as she slowly shakes her head.

"I don't think so, Sita," she says.

She turns and walks away.

I am left alone with my daughter's ashes, and soon these are gone, too, on the gentle ripples of the bay. I poured them from the vase without words, but with great nostalgia and love. True, she was an avatar, a creature of the divine, yet even Kalika's ashes dissolve in water. My memories are strong then, my pain nailed to a bloody past. But strong also is my vision of the future. It is true what Suzama says. I will leave this place, leave my few friends, and confront an enemy I know will kill me. Kill me because I crave love instead of power. But this I have lived five thousand years to learn. Power is as cold as forgotten ashes. Only my love can keep alive the memory of my daughter, the stories of Ray, Arturo, Yaksha, and most of all the grace of Krishna.

My blessed Lord—how he must laugh at me when I sing him to sleep in the middle of the night. Sing him songs from the holy Vedas that he himself wrote when he walked under the trees of ancient India. It is the divine child I will miss the most. Not to see him grow old, to hear him speak wisdom. I fear I will be ash before he even utters his first words. And I have to wonder who will remember me when I am gone. I worry that even Suzama and Seymour will forget me. Me—Alisa, Sita, or a thousand other names that I have been called by strangers who became friends or lovers. I fear it will be as if I never was. Never a vampire. The last vampire, whose long life now comes to a close.

Death does not scare me, but oblivion does. There is a difference. In my daughter's ashes I see my own bright star sink beneath the surface and go out. My end will erase my beginning. I don't know how but I know it is true. And I must choose that end because it is my destiny.

3

The wallet and the passport from Heidi's pockets identified her as a certain Linda Clairee. I know her address, her bank account number, even her supposed birthdate. She is supposed to have lived in a house not far from where I lived when I gave birth to Kalika. I am very curious as I drive to her house after flying into LAX.

The place is modest, nondescript even, stucco walls with a wooden fence surrounding an uninspired yard of grass and a few bushes. Slowly I walk toward the front door. There is someone inside watching TV and drinking what smells like beer. The sounds and odors drift out through a torn screen door. I knock lightly and brace myself for instant death. Yet I have a matrix

29

in my pocket, and I have finally figured out how to operate the ray gun. It is a totally cool weapon.

A bearded fellow in a frayed T-shirt answers the door. He looks as if he's on his second six-pack. Twenty-five, at most, his gut hangs over his belt like a sausage off the side of a breakfast plate. But I warn myself that Heidi—Linda—appeared to be very ordinary until her psychic force field went up. This guy might be more than he appears, but it's hard to believe.

"Hello," I say. "Is Linda home?"

He burps. "She's out of town."

At least he doesn't know she's missing her head.

"My name is Alisa," I say. "I'm an old friend. Do you know when she'll be back?"

"She didn't say."

"OK." I catch his eye through the screen door and squeeze his neuron currents. "Would it be OK if I come in and search through her personal things?"

His brain is soft mud, easy to impress—I think. "Sure," he says, and opens the door for me.

"Thank you," I respond.

I leave him in the living room, watching a baseball game. But my ears never leave him. If he tries to sneak up on me, he'll fail. But I won't kill him, if he shows strange powers, not right away.

Linda's room is neat and tidy. She seemed to enjoy sewing and the Dodgers. And if I begin to think I have the wrong house, there are pictures of her and Brother Bud on the mirror on top of the chest of drawers, cheap Polaroids shot with a camera with a dusty lens. Heidi is Linda and I am in the right bedroom. In each of the pictures Linda smiles as if someone just told her to.

I search the drawers and find nothing important. Even the closet is boring—clothes and baseball caps, shoes and socks. And this is the creature who said we all have powers? Talk about a double life. I am on the verge of leaving when a stack of papers under the bed catches my eye.

They are all about UFOs.

Specifically, newsletters from a UFO foundation.

FOF—Flying Objects Foundation.

What happened to the unidentified? I don't care. All the newsletters are addressed to Linda Clairee. She was definitely a member of this group, and it is the only wrinkle in her ordinary life that I have found. Holding the papers in my hand, I return to the living room and Bud. He is, in fact, finishing a can of Budweiser as I walk in. I turn off the TV without asking his permission and sit down across from him.

"Hey," he says, annoyed.

I catch his eye and burn a tiny hole in his frontal lobes. It will probably do him good, in the long run.

"Where did Linda say she was going?" I ask.

He replies in a flat voice, staring straight ahead. "Phoenix."

"What's in Phoenix?"

"A convention."

"A UFO convention?"

"Yes. FOF."

"Did Linda often attend such conventions?"

"Yes."

"Why?"

He could be hypnotized. "She likes UFOs."

"Why?"

"I don't know."

"Are you interested in UFOs?"

"No."

"Does Linda believe UFOs exist?"

"Yes."

"Is she an alien?"

"What?"

"Is Linda an alien creature?"

"No."

"Are you sure?"

"Sure, I'm sure."

"When did you meet Linda?"

"Three years ago."

"Where?"

"In a bar in Fullerton."

"What does Linda do for a living?"

"She works as a secretary."

"Have you ever been to her place of work?"

"Yes."

"Where is it?"

"In Fullerton. On Commonwealth and Harbor. Crays DP Office."

"What is Linda like?"

"Nice. Boring. Sexy."

"What is it like to have sex with her?"

"Fun. Always the same."

"What's your name?"

"Bill."

"What do you do for a living, Bill?"

"Drive a truck."

"Have you ever noticed anything unusual about Linda?"

"What do you mean?"

"Besides attending UFO conventions, does she do anything else odd?"

"Yes."

"What?"

"She stares at the sky at night a lot."

"How often?"

"Every night."

"Does she tell you why?"

"No."

"Do you ask?"

"No."

"When do you expect her back?"

"In two days."

"The convention runs until then?"

"Yes, I think."

"Does Linda have any family?"

"No. They are all dead."

"Every one of them?"

"Yes. Everyone."

"Bill, I am going to leave now but I might be back later. Until I return, I want you to forget I was ever here. I never existed. If someone should ask you if a stranger was here, just say no. Do you understand?"

"All right."

"Also, if Linda should fail to come home, don't worry about her. Get yourself another girl. She is not so important. Understand?"

"Yes."

"Good." I stand and step over and turn the TV back on. "Goodbye, Bill."

He glances up from the game. He doesn't even realize I interrupted it. "Goodbye," he says.

There is a plane leaving for Phoenix in fifty minutes and I get on it. Linda's newsletters have told me where the FOF convention is being held—a Holiday Inn beside a busy freeway. Once in Phoenix, I rent a Jeep and drive to the hotel, but all the rooms are taken. Taking a room at a nearby hotel, I shower and then go for a walk in the desert. Perhaps the UFO freaks took a hotel near the edge of town so they could look at the night sky. It is late—I study the stars as I walk, but nothing flies down from the sky to whisk me away. Yet I feel no pleasure beneath the heavens. A past I cannot remember haunts me.

"We are of an ancient tradition Our line is mingled with yours, and with that of others. We hold all powers."

Still, Linda wanted more of my blood, if she had any of it to begin with. Yet she must have had something unique. She was fast and strong, more powerful than virtually any vampire Yaksha made. Plus she had technology that put the government's most secret toys to shame. But so many of her answers had made no sense. What did she want to initiate me into?

"But to join us you must sacrifice him. It is part of your initiation."

It was almost as if she wanted to introduce me to the black mass.

I know about such things, sexual magic, from the past.

The torture and the blood, the sudden awakenings.

But I have not thought of them in a long time.

I find a sandy bluff and sit atop it to mentally survey my life, trying to find a point where my blood could have been taken without my knowledge. But except for Arturo and his alchemy, I think, my blood has always been mine to do with as I chose. Yet a faint feeling of dread sweeps over me as I look back. My shadow is long and dark. In it could lie secrets, hidden from even me, where blood was exchanged and vows were pledged that my conscious memory never recorded. It is as if I sense a blank spot, a place of reality that wasn't real after all. But I only sense its existence—I don't see it. I have to wonder if my imagination leads me to a wall of illusion. My thoughts are never far from those I left behind in Tahoe: John, Seymour, Paula. But Paula swears they are safe there, for now, and she should know. She who has deep visions.

A shooting star crosses the sky and I make a wish.

"Krishna," I whisper, "don't let me die until I have set right what I made wrong."

Suzama's words are with me. God's plan.

Somehow I know it was me who messed it up.

Maybe that's what she had been trying to tell me.

Maybe that was why she sent me away.

4

The next morning I am at the FOF convention in the Holiday Inn, milling around the many booths, poking my head in on lectures. The attendance is substantial, at least two thousand people. The crowd is pretty evenly divided between males and females, but otherwise the cross section is peculiar. There are, for want of a better expression, a lot of nerds here. Many are overweight and wear thick glasses. These are true believers, no doubt about it. The saucers are coming and they are prepared. In fact, they believe they are already here. Eavesdropping on their jumbled thoughts, I soon get a headache.

I sense no superbeings in the vicinity, yet I don't drop my guard. If this convention was important to Linda, there is somebody significant here. If only I knew who. Besides thoughts, I listen to heartbeats, trying to find physiologies that mimic mine. But there is nothing here but pure humanity.

The talks are boring, discussions of different sightings that have about as much credibility as reports of Santa Claus or the Easter Bunny. As I sit through one, yawning, I think about what I should have done with my life. Retired to a remote spot to spend a year building toys and baking goodies, which I would deliver once a year to the needy. At least then I could have given vampires a better name.

Yet there is a lecture at the end of the day that catches my eye. It is entitled: "Control Versus Anarchy—An Interstellar Dilemma." The speaker is to be Dr. Richard Stoon, a parapsychologist from Duke University. He has a list of impressive academic credentials beside his name, but it is really the buzz of the crowd that draws me to the talk. They have been waiting for this guy. I hear them whispering to one another. Dr. Stoon is supposed to be brilliant, charismatic, unorthodox. It is the last lecture of the convention, and I take a seat at the back of the audience and wait for Dr. Stoon to enter.

Beside me sits a pale blond woman, with a waist as small as my own, and clear blue eyes. She has a kind smile and I quickly scan her mind, detecting nothing more than a day job at a boring office, and a husband who has just been laid off. She appears to be in her early twenties but could be older. Noticing my scrutiny, she glances over and brightens.

"Hello," she said with a southern accent. "It's been a fun convention, hasn't it?"

"I haven't been here for the whole thing. I just caught today."

"Have you heard Dr. Stoon speak before?"

"This will be my first time. What's he like?"

"Very forceful, opinionated." She pauses. "He's interesting but to tell the truth he is awfully arrogant."

"Why don't you leave then?" I ask.

She makes a face. "Oh, I couldn't do that. I'm one of those people who has to see everything." She pauses and studies me. There is a sparkle in her eyes; she is far from stupid, but she doesn't want people to know. She offers her hand. "I'm Stacy Baxter."

I shake. "Alisa Perne. Pleased to meet you." I give one of my more common aliases because I'm no longer trying to hide. I want to draw the enemy out.

"Very pleased to meet you," Stacy replies. "I don't think I've seen you around before?"

"This is my first UFO convention."

"So what do you think?"

"It's all very interesting."

Stacy laughs. "No, you don't! You think we're all crackers."

Crackers. I haven't heard that expression in twenty years.

I have to smile. "I don't think you're crackers, Stacy."

She's pleased. "Maybe we can have coffee together after Dr. Stoon's talk."

"I'd enjoy that," I reply.

Dr. Stoon enters a short time afterward. He is a big burly man, of Slavic descent, with dark piercing eyes. His age, like Stacy's, is difficult to pinpoint. He could be thirty-five, or ten years older. He moves as if he owns the room, as if every eye should be on him. After a brief introduction, he is at the podium, overpowering it with his bulk and attitude. His voice, when he speaks, is gruff and unpleasant. Yet he sounds smart, like someone who knows more than he is saying.

And his words sound strikingly familiar.

"There are two kinds of beings in this creation," he says. "Those who strive for perfection and those who submit to chaos. It is the same in outer space as it is on this world—there is no difference. We either choose to be masters of our destinies, or we let the fates rule us. I am speaking now about power, and you might wonder what power has to do with a lecture on UFOs. I tell you it has everything to do with our space brothers. Each night we look to the heavens, waiting for them to arrive. But why should they come if we haven't made a choice in our own lives? But when we do make the choice, the right choice, to be important in the galactic scheme of things, then they will know. They will come to us at the most unexpected time, and fill our hands and minds with knowledge we cannot begin to imagine."

Stacy leans over and speaks in my ear. "Sounds like a bit of an evangelist, doesn't he?"

"Yeah. He talks without saying anything specific."

Stacy nodded. "But look at the people in this room. They are spellbound. Dr. Stoon doesn't have to say anything to have the effect he wants."

Stacy misunderstands me, but her point is well made. Dr. Stoon is one of those people who draws others in, smothers them. Even though he's not being specific, he touches on issues Suzama—and that's who she will always be to me—also explained. Yet his bias is from the other side, even though nothing he says sounds intrinsically negative.

He continues in a loud voice.

"We have to open our minds fully to the truth that we control our own futures, while at the same time we must accept that there are powers above us that are willing to help us if we align our thinking with theirs. Who are our space brothers? They are us a thousand years from now. They are strong. And for us to be strong we must cut off all that weakens us as a people. Here I have to speak on a matter that is almost considered a blasphemy in our society, and yet it is the single most important issue regarding our survival. We are literally drowning in the shallow end of our gene pool. Who is reproducing at the most rapid rate in our world? The uneducated and the foolish. But how did our space brothers reach their exalted state? By casting out the foolish. Our genes are our only treasure. We must plan their use, and use the plan—the plan our brothers are waiting to give us."

Again Stacy leans over and whispers in my ear.

"Sounds like Hitler to me," she says.

I smile. "But he's not blaming any specific group for mankind's woes."

"Isn't he?" Stacy asks, and her question is worth contemplating.

Dr. Stoon speaks for another half hour, and at the end of that time he doesn't accept questions—probably because no one would know what to ask him. I certainly wouldn't. Yet his words have affected me, not so much by their content, but by their resonance. I don't know, however, if the effect is a good one. His lecture was divisive; nothing he said could be used to bring people together for the common good. Another might say that was not true. Such was the strength and weakness of his talk.

When he finishes I wander toward the front, where

he stands chatting with what appear to be old friends. But when his eyes meet mine, he momentarily freezes, and then quickly turns away. He excuses himself from his group and walks briskly toward the exit.

I walk after him.

In the parking lot he climbs in his car and races out onto the road, heading for the desert. Naturally I follow him. He must know I am tailing him. At this time of day, a half hour after dusk, we are the only ones on this narrow road that runs perpendicular to the main highway. Within twenty minutes we are deep in the desert, with the city only a glow on the horizon. The stars come out. Dr. Stoon is driving fast, but now it is possible he may not know I am behind him. I have turned off my headlights. I don't need them, of course, but maybe he doesn't either.

Ten minutes later he suddenly swerves off the road and drives across the sand toward a massive hill that is more reminiscent of Utah's Zion National Park than Phoenix's backyard. The hill is more a stone cathedral, built around a symmetrical interior. The rough terrain is hard on Dr. Stoon's BMW but my Jeep loves the challenge.

He drives his car as close to the hill as he can, then stops and gets out.

What do I do? I realize I could be walking into a trap. If he has a matrix, as I have, he could incinerate my Jeep from a distance. I have experimented with the weapon—it has a substantial range. The way he fled from me, for no apparent reason, indicates he is more than he seems. Yet his exit was obvious as well. But I sense no one else in the area, and I can hear a snake slither at a distance of five miles in such a desert.

I decide to risk direct confrontation.

Dr. Stoon stands with his arms at his sides as I drive up. Slowly I climb from my Jeep, the matrix in hand. I do not wish to waste time on pretense. If he is like Linda, he is going to do some talking. If he is human, he has a funny way of showing it. Either way I believe he will die in this desert tonight. I may even drink his blood, although I have not fed from anyone since Kalika brought me back from the edge of death. My hunger simply seems to have vanished. I gesture with my weapon. A million stars shine down on us. I see them all, more than a mortal can see with a medium-size telescope.

"Move away from the car," I say. "Put your hands in the air."

He does as I command. "What do you want?" he asks in a much softer voice than he used at the convention. I step closer.

"I should ask you that question, Dr. Stoon," I say. "What do you want?"

He does not hesitate. "We told you."

"You told me little. Who are you people?"

He smiles slightly, cocky bastard. "Who do you think?"

"Extraterrestials."

"You are partially right, and partially wrong. We have been here a long time."

"How long?"

"Don't you remember?"

His question disturbs me, his voice. I realize he is trying to overpower me with his eyes. His are at least as strong as Linda's. Try as I might, I cannot pierce his aura to read his mind.

"I remember nothing of you. Answer my question."

"Over a thousand years," he says.

"Where did you come from? Originally?"

"There is no simple answer to that question. We move in space and time, through dimensions and distortions."

"Are you here to distort humanity?"

"We are here for the harvest."

"For which side of the harvest?"

"There is only one side—the expansion of the self, the growth of self-awareness."

"Sounds nice. But at whose expense?"

He snorts. "The expense of all those too weak to move forward. Why do you ask these questions? We know you are a vampire, the most powerful vampire on Earth. We have watched you for centuries. You do what you wish; we do as we wish. We are brothers to you, sisters. Why don't you join us?"

"It doesn't sound like you want me as a brother or sister. It sounds like you want me as a blood bank." I pause. "Or do you already have some of my blood?"

He makes me wait. "We do," he says finally.

I stiffen. The confirmation wounds me.

"When?" I ask. I feel violated.

"Over a thousand years ago."

"When?" I demand.

He gloats. "Kalot Enbolot. Chateau Merveille." He pauses before he says the next words. "The Castle of Wonder."

I tremble, not just in my body, but in my very soul.

In all my long life, there had never been darker days.

Yet I thought I had escaped his aerie unscathed.

"Landulf," I whisper. "Oh God."

Dr. Stoon grins. "Landulf took the best you had to

give, now we will take it again. With or without your assistance."

I back up involuntarily. "You lie!" I gasp. "He never touched me!"

Dr. Stoon speaks with scorn. "He did more than touch you. He bled you, used you, and then twisted your mind so that you didn't know. But don't you remember now, Sita? As you swam through the waves away from his castle? Swam to what you thought was freedom? Even the ocean water could not wash off the contamination you felt then. Yet you thought you had won, defeated him. Just as you think you will defeat us now."

I cannot stop shaking. The images his words invoke—I cannot bear to see them in my suddenly shattered mind. Landulf and his sexual magic, satanic practice that used terror and pain for fuel. The human sacrifices, bodies split open with dirty knives, and worst of all the spirits that would appear at his bidding, vicious creatures from an astral hell buried beneath unheeded cries. From the Temple of Erix at which the Priestess of Antiquity had once guarded the Oracle of Venus, in southwest Sicily, he sent forth these unclean spirits and dominated the minds and hearts of men and women throughout southern Europe. Inviting the hordes of invading Moslems, showing them the weaknesses in the Christian world's defenses and so betraying his own race, Landulf had changed the course of history in the ninth century. And so he had changed my life, putting a stain on it that more than ten centuries had not totally erased. I tremble for many reasons, all of them unbearable. Landulf had indeed touched me, I remember, kissed me even, with lips that often enjoyed raw human flesh.

Yet I still thought I had tricked him.

"I will defeat you," I whisper without conviction. "If you have anything to do with him, I will not rest until all of your kind are wiped out. Landulf was a demon, and you use his name as if he were a hero. Your power is a travesty." I aim the matrix. "You will all die."

Dr. Stoon grins and lowers his hands. "We are not alone."

I glance left and right, see nothing, hear only the desert.

Yet I sense the truth of his words, sense a presence.

"Tell them to show themselves," I say carefully. "If you want to live one second longer."

"Very well." He bows his head slightly.

Suddenly there are three figures in red robes, one on each side, another at my back. Each carries a matrix in his or her hand, although their faces are shadowed, as are their minds. They are humanoid but that is all I know about them. They have me in their sights. There seems to be no escape. Dr. Stoon sticks out his hand.

"The matrix, please," he says.

I shake my head. "I will vaporize myself before you will have my blood."

He is amused. "Try."

I try the weapon on him. But it doesn't work.

"We neutralized it at the convention," he explains.

I throw the weapon aside. "You don't want me dead."

"True," he says. "But we will kill you before we allow you to kill us. Lay facedown on the sand."

"I hardly think so," I say, and my attention goes to the figure on my right, the one whose hand shakes ever so slightly. This person—I cannot even see his eyes—but I know it is a male, weaker than the others that guard me. Even though I cannot read his mind, I can sense the general character of it. This is an important assignment for him, one that he has had to struggle to win. If he completes it successfully, captures the vampire's blood, he will receive some type of advancement. But if he fails, he will be killed. Indeed, he is especially fearful of Dr. Stoon. He wishes the doctor dead. That is the chink in his psychic armor. He does not care for his associates, hates them in fact, wishes they all were dead so that all the glory could be his. My eyes fasten on his hidden face, my thoughts drill into his cranium.

Kill them. Burn them. Vanquish them.

The man's arm trembles more.

"It is not wise to refuse us," Dr. Stoon says.

"Do you still give me a chance to join you?" I mutter, stalling for time. Never before have I focused so hard, called upon the depths of my will. The strain is immense. For even though this one is the weakest, he is still strong beyond belief.

"Perhaps," Dr. Stoon says. "Lay facedown or die. Now."

"Die," I repeat softly, to the man. "Die."

His aim shifts slights. The finger on the button on his matrix twitches.

Dr. Stoon is suddenly aware of the danger. He whirls on the man.

"Kill him!" he screams.

There are two bursts of red light, one from behind

me, one from my left. My victim vaporizes on an ear-piercing scream. But I do not pause to mourn the sound. I am already in the air, flipping backward in a curving arc, my legs going over me, carrying me over the assailant at my rear. There is another burst of red death—the one on my left tries to shoot me out of the sky. But already I have landed, behind the one who moments earlier stood behind me. In a matter of microseconds I seize his matrix and break his arm. Without speaking, I blow away the red robe on the left. Dr. Stoon reaches into his coat pocket but I caution him to remain still.

"Don't," I say.

The figure I have disarmed groans, moves.

I shoot him and he is no more.

Dr. Stoon has stopped grinning.

"How many more of you are there?" I ask.

He pauses. "There is just me."

"And when you die, you die?"

He hesitates. "We prefer not to surrender this form."

I chuckle. "I do believe there is a note of fear in your voice, good doctor. For a moment there, you know, I thought you were Landulf himself. But Landulf was never afraid."

"Not even of you," he says bitterly.

"Yes," I say sadly, thinking of what he has told me. "Perhaps I was tricked. What did he use my blood for?"

"Is it not obvious?"

"Only your death is obvious. Answer my question so that death won't catch you asking."

He is defiant. "I will not be your puppet. We are

alone for the moment, but others of my kind are coming. And if you should slay me, their treatment of you will be that more hideous."

I shake my head. "Nothing can be hideous to me. Not after Landulf."

He speaks arrogantly. "You will not escape us."

"Really? You thought I wouldn't escape you."

He doesn't have an answer for that.

I shoot him and he troubles me no more.

5

I return to my Jeep and drive back toward the road. When I reach it there is another car waiting for me, another person. She stands by the side of the road looking up at the stars. She hardly seems to notice my approach, and only glances over as I park and walk toward her, the matrix in my hand.

Stacy Baxter. She finally glances at me and smiles.

"Hello, Alisa," she says, and the southern accent is gone.

My finger is on the fire button. "What are you doing here?" I ask softly.

She shrugs and gazes back up at the sky. "Just enjoying the night. Isn't it beautiful?"

"Yes. Did you follow me out here?"

She pauses. "Yes."

"I see." I am a moment away from killing her. "Do you have anything else to say, Stacy Baxter?"

She looks at me again, not smiling now, just watching me, very closely. "No, Alisa Perne," she replies quietly.

I shift uncomfortably. This death does not feel right.

"Are you one of them?" I ask finally.

She shakes her head. "Not me."

"Who are you?"

"A friend."

"No. I don't know you." I shake the weapon. "Why are you here?"

"To help you, if you want my help."

"What's your real name?"

"Alanda," she replies. "Sita."

My heart pounds. "And you are another incantation of Lundulf's?"

Sorrow touches her face. "You suffered there."

I bite my lip. "Yeah, I suffered. But what's it to you?"

She lowers her head. "Everything you have experienced—it means a lot to me."

My voice is hard. "Why? Because you know me from long ago?"

"Yes."

I fidget on my feet. I want to kill her. Logic dictates that I should. This desert is filled with monsters. Chances are she is one, too. Certainly she is not normal, and knows too much about me. Yet she does nothing to defend herself, even to plead her case, and I find it difficult to strike down the helpless.

"Do you know this weapon I carry?" I ask.

"Yes."

"I know how to use it." I pause. "I will use it."

Alanda is staring at the stars again. "Then use it."

"You are impossible. I will kill you, just as I killed the others out there minutes ago. You saw that, didn't you?"

"Yes."

I am sarcastic. "Why didn't you come to my aid? Friend?"

"It was not allowed."

"By whom?" I demand.

"You had to refuse them. To offer to end your life before they would take it from you." She adds, "You did these things."

"I did nothing but kill. Because they answered me the same way you do, with vague mumblings." I pause and sweat over the trigger. "I think you are one of them."

For the third time she looks at me, and for the first time I really see her. Her blue eyes—they are very much like my own. I could be staring into a mirror. Yet it is more than a physical resemblance. The person behind the eyes, the soul within the body, seems to reach out and touch me in a way I cannot explain. For a moment—from this unassuming person I am threatening to destroy—I feel profoundly cherished. Suddenly she is more than a friend to me, she is a part of me. Sometimes when I looked at Suzama, I would feel this way. Occasionally, gazing at the divine child, I would sense this same expansion of consciousness, as if my mind were only a portion of a much greater mind. It is only in that moment that I realize Alanda is a spiritual being of great stature, someone who loves me more than I am able to love myself.

The matrix slips from my fingers, lands in the sand. A tear rolls over my cheek and joins it in the dust. I don't know why I cry, perhaps because I am happy. Alanda *is* an old friend.

Yet I don't remember her.

As I don't remember Landulf stealing my blood.

"I don't understand," I whisper.

She comes to me and hugs me, stroking my face. "Sita," she says over and over again. "My Sita."

But I am not a child. I am a monster. I cannot be comforted even if the space between us is suffused with the vitality of reunion. I cannot turn to this creature that I do not know for help or solace. In a swift move, I brush her off and step away, turning my back on her. If she wanted, she could pick up the matrix and vaporize me. But I know that is not her intention. She lets me stand silently alone. Nothing is hurried in her, I realize. She has waited long for this encounter, and I feel I have as well. Yet I feel exposed before her, and that is a feeling I have never enjoyed. I have always been the master of my own destiny, and now this angelic being comes to me in the night to tell me that I have been fooling myself. Truly, she is an angel to me, a being of light from a distant world I cannot imagine.

"There is no need for imagination," she says quietly. "Those worlds belong to you as much as to me."

I draw in a tight breath. "You are telepathic then?"

"Yes. As are you."

"No. I cannot read your mind."

"You can. You're just afraid, Sita."

"How do you know my name?"

"Because I know you."

"From when? From where?"

"From before. From the stars."

A smile cracks my face, involuntarily. Turning, almost mocking her, I say, "Where's your spaceship?"

"It's coming."

That remark makes me take a step back.

"Are you here to take me away?" I ask, and I hear the hope in my own voice. For five thousand years, I have lived a glorious life, yet there has been too much pain. Alanda's love seems to flow to me in waves. The desert is dry, her eyes are moist. I cannot help but be mesmerized by them, by all of her. She is shimmering now with a faint blue light.

This blue glow, it reminds me of Krishna.

The stars. How bright they shine above us.

Almost as if they have moved closer to Earth.

But Alanda's face is both blissful and concerned.

"No," she says. "You cannot leave this world now, not until what has been ruined has been set right."

"Suzama said as much. Do you know her?"

"Yes. She is a sister, like you."

"Suzama is much more than I am."

"You are fond of denouncing yourself."

"I haven't been a saint exactly. You must know that."

"Yes. But that is past. You are here with me now, and I am with you."

My throat is constricted. "I feel you with me, yes."

"Why are you afraid of love, Sita? Because it has hurt you?"

I nod weakly. "It hurts all of us. Sometimes it seems that is all love is good for."

Alanda shakes her head. "Love is good for many things. You have just forgotten. The veil has to be lifted."

I am curious. "What is this veil?"

Alanda turns away and walks on the sand, between the weeds. She is barefoot—I only realize that now. The way her soles touch the ground, it is almost as if they caress the Earth. Gesturing at the desert, the stars, and playing with her long blond hair, she enchants me as she speaks. The communication may even be telepathic, her voice is so soft. But it is easy to understand her.

"This galaxy is ancient, as you know," she says. "Your sun is old, but the stars at the center of the galaxy were there first. The planets circling them gave rise to civilizations. So life evolved. First plants, then animals and finally, what you would call people arrived. Some of these people looked like us, but not all. They became conscious. They knew all that the people of this world know, and more. For there was at that time no veil between the conscious and the unconscious, no loss of the awareness that we are all a part of the creation. The gods of those suns did not desire this veil to confuse their children, and therefore everyone on those ancient planets lived in light and peace. Do you understand?"

"I'm not sure," I say. "Continue."

"Suzama has told you about the coming harvest, on this world. These ancient people also arrived at a point when it was important for them to move on, to move into another realm, a fourth dimension if you like. But then there was a problem. All these beings from the central suns of this galaxy were positive— what you would call good-hearted. But because they had always lived in bliss, they had no incentive to grow. Therefore, for many billions of years, from the third dimension to the fourth, there were few harvests. Such people were a rarity." Alanda pauses. "Do you understand?"

"Yes. The source of pain for us—here on this world—is the veil between the conscious and the unconscious. Yet this pain acts as a catalyst for us to grow."

"Precisely. People of your world often speak of good and evil. But what you call evil goads you onto the greatest good. This is necessary for you, and all people of your world. That is why it is there. That is why the great being within your sun allows the veil to exist. The story from the Garden of Eden—the knowledge of good and evil that your ancient ancestors received—that was not a curse but a blessing. It only seems a curse to you at times like this, when you are in doubt."

"But to some extent we live our whole lives in doubt." I pause. "So you're saying the devil wasn't such a bad guy after all?"

"No. I am saying there is a place for negativity—as much as there is a place for goodness—in the great scheme of things. There is no hero without a villain, no peak without a valley. But our path, the path of love, demands that we overcome negativity. But we do not overcome it by resisting it. That is an illusion. What you resist will persist."

"Why are you telling me this?" I ask, and there is suddenly fear in my voice. But I know what she will answer. For I knew, personally, the greatest evil that ever walked the Earth. Still, Alanda's words chill me to the bone.

"Landulf cannot be overcome by force," she says.

My lower lip trembles. "Landulf is dead. He died a long time ago."

"Perhaps. Perhaps not. But certainly his work lives on. You met a sample of it tonight in the desert. There are more of them emerging at this time, and they possess a sample of your blood." She steps toward me, looks at me. "Do you know what that means?"

I snort. "Yeah. It means they're tough sonsof-bitches."

Alanda is serious. "Yes. They are tough. And it was never intended that the negative side of harvest should possess such a powerful army of warriors. In the coming years they will overwhelm your people, turn virtually everyone toward fear. This will be the downfall for all who aspire to the light. This fear will cause the negative harvest to be larger than it would have been. In other words, your world is out of balance."

"And I caused this imbalance?"

Alanda sighs. "This must be difficult for you to hear."

"The truth is always better than illusions." I pause. "Is it true?"

"Yes. You are the ultimate source of this cancer, and it must be rectified."

"Are you so sure?" I ask, trying to deny what I just heard. It's too much for me, to be told that I am the scourge of mankind. I feel as if I must run away. Only my irrational love for her makes me stay.

Alanda is gentle. Her next word is not. "Yes."

"But how can you be sure?" I demand.

"Because my old and dear friend, I am from your future."

I take a moment to absorb her statement. "What is it like?"

Now she stutters. "In ruins."

I am shocked. "This world?"

The life leaves her voice. "This entire sector of the galaxy. When so much of Earth fails, much else fails later." Alanda steps close to me, puts her hands on my shoulders, her eyes in my soul. "We have come back for you, Sita, to ask you to help us. To ask you to go back to the days of Landulf. To relive those days, and keep him from doing to you what he desired."

The prospect fills me with horror. "But I can't remember what he did to me!"

"You will, I promise, when you travel back to that time."

"No." I shake my head, feeling my guts turn to ice. "That is one thing I cannot do. Ask anything of me but that."

Alanda strokes the side of my face. "You are afraid."

Again I brush her off and turn aside. "Yes," I say in a shaky voice. "And I don't understand why. I can't understand why the simple thought of seeing him again overwhelms me."

"It's because of what you can't remember."

I whirl around. "Then tell me what happened?"

"I cannot. You must face the memory when you are once more in his castle. It is the only way. It is why he was able to block your memory in the first place. At that time you refused to face what happened."

"Did he torture me? Did he mutilate me?"

She nods reluctantly. "In his own way. But there is more than that to the puzzle—you will see."

I am sick at the prospect. "Is your spaceship a time machine as well?"

Alanda glances up. "Not exactly."

"But how can I go back to those days? How can I meet myself?"

She stares at me. "Physically you will not journey in time. Only your mind will go back."

"I don't understand?"

"As our ships approach light speed, we are able to jump into a realm that exists outside time and space. In that realm we can cross many light-years in a moment. The enemy also has this technology, and that is how they were able to surround you in the desert tonight. In that realm, the laws of physics as you understand them do not apply. For a few seconds you will cease to exist in a particular time and place. Therefore, you will have the freedom to be where you wish to be. If you focus all your will on that ninth century vampire, you will become her. Do you see?"

"No. Will both our minds be in the same body?"

"No. There is only one of you. You will become her, and she will become you. There is no question of two."

I am still confused, but dread continues to dominate my mind. "I can't see him again," I plead. "You don't know what he was like."

Alanda is sad. "But I know his kind well. He is not from the dimension beyond this one, but from the one even beyond that. He is negative fifth density— not merely a sorcerer, but a master of sorcerers. Above his head the vipers hiss, and before his vision all wills turn to stone. Those you met tonight are only his minions. But he is not greater than you, Sita. I know you, old friend, know of your extraordinary origin. You cannot directly resist him when you confront him, for in doing so you will become him.

That is his special power, the spell he cloaked you in before. Yet you can defeat him." Quoting Suzama, she adds, " 'Faith is stronger than stone.' "

"But you will not tell me how to defeat him?"

"No. You must find the way. It is your destiny to do so."

I don't want to ask the question but I do anyway.

"Is it also my destiny to die? Alanda?"

She shakes her head. "I cannot say."

"But you come from the future. You know. Tell me."

"I know that you will rewrite our future. Please do not ask me to say more." Her eyes return to the heavens and she points. "Behold, Sita. Our ship comes for you."

6

The funny thing is, I don't see anything. Alanda explains that the ship will land deep in the desert, beside a clear pond. She offers to drive me there, but I prefer to take the Jeep, so she goes with me instead. We cut directly across the sand, murdering more than a few tumbleweeds in the process. Yet the ground is not excessively bumpy, and we soon reach the pond. After parking, I climb out and stare at it in amazement.

The pond appears to be natural—Alanda assures me it is even though it is a perfect circle. A hundred feet across, the water lies so still that it could be a polished mirror set to reflect the stars. Indeed, as I approach the edge of the pond, I see more stars in the water than I do above. I see the approach of the saucer in the water before I see it in the sky, quite a few seconds before. It makes me wonder, yet I say nothing.

The saucer is blue-white, and the light from it slowly begins to flood the area and my eyes, wiping out any chance of my making out the details. If I weren't dreading seeing Landulf, I would be thrilled by this moment. But I can only think of Landulf's devishly handsome face, his deep laugh, and the way he would make an incision in an abdomen with his long sharp nails and slowly pull out the victim's entrails while the victim watched. I feel I must resist Landulf with every fiber of my being. Yet Alanda says that is the way of failure.

I have no idea what I'll do that is different from what I did the last time.

I stare up at the saucer.

"This is incredible," I whisper.

"This is but a beam ship," she says. "Our mother ships are a thousand times this size."

"And I have been on these before?"

"Yes."

"When?"

"Another time."

"Are you sure the brakes work? The ship looks as if it's going to land on us."

"It will land over this pool."

"Then we should move?"

"No. We're fine. It will move right over us."

The light grows dazzling, and I have to shield my eyes.

"This must be visible from a hundred miles away," I gasp.

"No one sees it but us," Alanda replies.

I glance at her. "Is it physical?"

"What is physical in one density is not physical in another."

I have to laugh. "One of these days, Alanda, I am going to ask you a question and understand your answer."

The water of the pond seems to glow as the spaceship settles over us. One moment it is above us, the next we are inside it. The translucent floor, I assume, now covers the pond. During the move to the interior, we have had our clothes changed. We now wear long white robes. I don't even bother asking—the night is so weird already.

A gentleman waits for us inside. He is tall and bearded—like a child's drawing of a Biblical character. His robe is the color of the outside of the ship, blue-white. The interior of the vessel is in various shades of gold, and the ceiling is a clear dome, that opens to the sky. There appear to be no controls. Alanda introduces her friend as Gaia. He smiles and bows his head but doesn't say anything. His eyes are liquid green and very lovely.

"Gaia is from a race that doesn't speak," Alanda explains. "But he understands your thoughts."

I nod in his direction. "I appreciate your coming for us, Gaia. I hope it was not too long a journey."

He smiles and shakes his head. No, not too long.

There is a faint humming.

"What is that?" I ask.

"Our engines," Alanda says.

"Will we leave soon?"

"We have already left." Alanda motions with her arm. "See, we are in orbit."

The floor of the craft turns clear as glass, and I jump slightly, momentarily afraid I am going to fall. Below our feet is the black-blue Pacific, and the glittering coast of California. I spot Lake Tahoe, and think of my friends. We seem to be moving westward, at considerable speed. Yet the hum has stopped, and all is quiet. The view takes my breath away, it is so beautiful, and yet it also makes me sad. To see the Earth from such a vantage point, to realize it is all I have known. Never before did I realize how much I thought of the Earth as my mother.

"She is a strong woman," Alanda says softly, reading my mind. "But delicate as well."

"Can a planet be alive?" I ask.

"Can a sun?" she replies. "I told you that it was the god within your sun that decided that humanity should live with the veil—until this time."

"Are you from a world that experienced such a veil?"

"Originally, yes."

"Can you tell me about that world?" I ask.

"Not at this time."

"But I lived there before I came to Earth?"

"Not precisely. Before you came here, you existed in a realm of great glory."

"You're saying that I was in a higher dimension?"

"Yes," Alanda says. "A higher density."

"Why did I decide to come to Earth?"

"To serve, to grow. The two are the same in the creator's eyes."

"Why did I chose to be a vampire?"

Alanda hesitates. "When you came here, you were not a vampire."

"I had a life before this one?"

Her voice is abruptly filled with melancholy. "Yes. Very long ago."

She is trying to tell me something without saying it.

"I made a mistake when I returned?" I say. "Is that why I had to be reborn as a vampire?"

Alanda reaches over and touches my face. "You returned to this third density out of love. If you made a mistake, Sita, it was only out of love. You mustn't blame yourself."

Already we are over India. I nod to Rajastan, desert meeting green.

"I was born there five thousand years ago," I say. "I am sure you know that. But what you might not know is that I feel I never left that tiny village. I am still that young girl spying on the Aghora sacrifice that invoked Yaksha into Amaba's dead womb." I pause. "I held him as an unborn infant in my hand. He was just a trace of movement beneath the hard skin of a corpse. I had a knife in my hand, and my father gave me the choice of ending his life before it could begin." A wave of weariness sweeps over me and I lower my head. "But I couldn't kill Yaksha."

Alanda hugs me. "Because of love, you see. You must let go of the past."

"But you are sending me into a past I want to let go of."

"But this is the only way you will be able to be finished with it. Trust us, Sita. We do this for you as much as for ourselves. Our futures are entwined."

I look up and smile. "Just because I almost killed you doesn't mean I believe you would lie to me." I pause. "You risked your life meeting me like that."

"It was the only way to meet you."

"It was a test?" I ask.

"In a manner of speaking."

"You could have defended yourself from me."

Alanda turns back to the view. "I counted on your compassion."

"The compassion of a murderer?"

"Of an angel."

I have to laugh. "You are as bad as Seymour. He sees me that way, no matter what I do."

"He is wise."

I sigh. "I would love it if he were with us now."

Alanda is thoughtful. "In a sense, he is. He is always with you."

Her remark strikes deeply into me. "Why is that so true?"

Alanda stares at the Earth, India. "You will see."

A short time later the Earth begins to shrink as we pull away from it at a tremendous velocity. Soon it is only a blue ball, falling into a well of blackness. The floor turns solid as the sides become clear. The rays of the sun stab through the saucer's view screens and I feel their warmth. There is no sense of acceleration, however. I see the moon, but only for a few seconds, and then it is lost in the glare of the Earth. But then that planet, the only home I can remember, is also lost in the rays of the sun. The sun begins to diminish in size and brilliance. Alanda turns away and strolls to the center of the craft. But my eyes are gripped by the stars ahead of us.

"I've had these dreams," I say to Alanda and Gaia both. Gaia stands at a respectful distance, silent, peaceful, absorbed in a contemplation I cannot imagine. Yet I know he watches me and listens to my thoughts. I continue, "In them I would be in a spaceship flying through the galaxy toward the Pleiades. Ray would usually be with me, but sometimes it would be my husband, Rama. Never were both with me, but I think that's because—in my dreams—they were always the same person. Anyway, we would be excited and filled with a sense of adventure. We would know, when we reached the Pleiades, that all our friends would be waiting for us. We even knew that Krishna would be there, to welcome us and to heal the many injuries we had received living on Earth. Most of all, in these dreams, I would be happy, and it would be hard to wake from them." I pause. "Were they just dreams, Alanda?"

"Or were they real?" she asks. "Maybe they were a little of both."

I look at her. "Are you from the Pleiades?"

"It is a place I know." She shrugs. "We are each from God."

I listen to the silence. "It's time, isn't it?"

"Yes. In a few minutes, we will make what you might call a hyperjump. At that time, as I explained before, it is important that you focus your entire being to a time just before you traveled to Landulf's castle."

"It was Dante who led me to the castle," I say, stepping toward her. "Should I think of him?"

Alanda pauses. "The moment you reappear is entirely up to you."

I force a smile, although the dread weighs on me like a stone in my heart.

"It will be good to see Dante again," I say. "A little comic relief before I descend into hell." I gesture to the center of the floor. "Should I sit down and close my eyes?"

Alanda takes my hand. "Lie down and close them, Sita."

I do as she says, but she continues to hold my hand. I open my eyes and smile at her. "Don't worry," I say. "It is just my mind that is going back in time."

She shakes her head slightly. "But if you die back then."

I understand. "I won't exist today?"

She sighs. "There is something else. These fifth density negative beings—they can imprison you."

"I'm pretty good at breaking out of most prisons."

"They can imprison your soul, in their realm. Make you one of them."

Somehow that doesn't sound fair. "For long?"

"Billions of years. You would only be set free when they are set free."

"Negative beings attain freedom?" I ask.

"Yes. Far up the ladder of evolution, the negative path meets the positive. In the end, all find God." She squeezes my hand. "But you could be lost for the life of this universe."

I cannot conceive of anything worse.

"How can he trap me?" I ask.

"He is subtle, and we cannot penetrate his mind. But he acts much as a mirror does. He stands before you. He shows you what you are. But only the parts of you that can be used to destroy you."

"He can cause me to destroy myself?"

"Exactly. Be wary. He can kill you without your permission. But he can only pervert you to his cause if you enter into an agreement with him out of free will."

"But I would never do that."

Alanda seems unsure. Her expression is anxious.

She leans over and kisses my cheek. There is a tear on her face and I reach up to wipe it away but she grabs my other hand.

"You are loved," she whispers. "Don't forget that."

"I know. I know you." I close my eyes. "Goodbye, Alanda."

"Sita. My Sita."

She lets go of me. The ship darkens.

I hear the strange hum again, a shift inside.

But inside, outside—they have lost their meaning.

We are beyond space and time, and I am falling.

Into horror unspeakable, yes, and maybe hope unimagined.

7

The collage of colors and shapes that I now see is my life. Yet the different scenes from it are not arranged in a linear fashion, more in the form of a hologram, a pictorial dimension of time that encircles me like a living sphere. I have only to focus my attention on a particular event and I am there. But perhaps because my mind is used to dealing with sequential events, I take myself back in order. This is my deliberate choice, not the choice of the creation. To the creation, I realize, everything is happening in the same eternal moment.

I am with my daughter, Kalika, holding her as she bleeds from devastating chest wounds. Her smile is gentle and I am crying. She tells me she loves me. Then I cry over Seymour, beside his funeral pyre, because Kalika has killed him. Yet a few drops of the divine child's blood and he is alive again. Then I am laughing. Tears are connected to laughter in my life. One seems to bring the other, and that in itself is a great mystery to me. Blood, also, is everywhere. I see the night my daughter was born, in pain and love. The opposites of all life fly before my expanded vision, yet they now seem to be in harmony with one another.

Arturo and Joel are beside me. They tell me they love me. There is a flash of blinding light. They die, their love kills them, I destroy them. But a moment later I am saving Joel by making him a vampire, and a moment before that I am reviving Ray by the same process. Then I take a leap and I am sitting beside Ray's father as he dies from a ferocious blow I have struck to his chest. He perishes with the fear that I will harm his son, the son I love. Again and again, my love brings danger and death.

The hologram of my life seems to spin. In quick succession I see Hitler screaming at his troops, Lincoln ordering General Grant to take up the Union's moral cause. Then I am in a castle in the highlands of Scotland, defending it from an evil duke. Once more my lover dies, and in the next instant I stand before the Inquisition, condemning Arturo to death. Arturo, who has meant more to me than practically anyone I have ever known. I see his eyes as I curse him, but I do not see his heart, do not know that he has already tricked me. I ensure his death but he does not die.

Finally I am walking in the dry hills of Sicily outside Messina, eating a bunch of purple grapes and wondering where I am heading. It is the ninth century and even the evening air is hot. This is my first visit to Sicily; the previous day I took a sailboat across the straits from Italy. Something about the land has drawn me to this spot in particular, but as of yet I don't know what. My long blond hair is pulled up under a cap, and I wear gray hose and a short linen tunic. I could be a pretty young boy, with my baggy white shirt and long steel knife tucked in my belt. The sun is in the sky, but it bothers me just a little.

Then I am not watching this other self.

I am her, and it isn't easy for either of us.

There is a moment of duality. She does not know me.

I feel as if I bump heads with a shadow, and yet my shadow thinks she is the real one, and that I am the ghost. It takes me a moment to explain, and the moment almost cracks open into an insane fissure of delusion. This Sita does not have a volume of my memories, and certainly does not know about flying saucers and the possibility of mental time travel. I am forced to impress these possibilities on her through a wall of internal resistance that threatens to explode both our minds. Then I realize it is hopeless, that I cannot force myself on myself. I relax, and back off, and then suddenly she is curious about me. She knows me even when she doesn't know all of me. I was always one for a new experience, and meeting myself along an empty road is about as weird an experience as I have ever had. My younger self calls to me.

"Ritorna da me," she says. Come back to me.

"Fa bene," I reply, aloud. All right.

Sita is startled. Who is talking to whom?

Her curiosity is greater than her fear.

I am able to get inside and there I stay.

Finally she understands. The duality ceases. I am Alisa Perne of the twentieth century, in the ninth century, here in Sicily to defeat a monster. There is only me but I am now of firm resolve. Landulf had better beware.

Around the bend of the next hill, I hear cries. Dante.

Before I had not known I would meet him, but now it is as if he is calling my name. Tossing aside my grapes, I run to an appointment I have with the past. Yet already I am not thinking of myself as from the future. Perhaps the other Sita is there as much as I. Yet I do notice that I am not nearly so fast as I was before. This body has not had the last infusions of powerful blood. I am just an ordinary vampire—I can't even read minds. All that I have, that I didn't have before, are memories of things that have not yet happened. They are my only new weapons against Landulf.

As I come around a hill, I find Dante naked and bleeding, strung up to a skeleton of a tree by a rope tied to his right arm and right foot. Gathered around him are two men and a woman, the two men holding swords and poking at poor Dante, encouraging him to sing. There is another rope around Dante's neck. The meaning is clear—if Dante stops singing, they will cut the other ropes and he will be hung.

Dante is not in good shape. At a glance I realize he has severe leprosy of his left arm and leg. The disease has actually eaten away portions of his bones, and I know he must live in terrible pain. He has also been castrated, but by the sweetness in his voice I recognize that he is no ordinary eunuch. He is a castrato, perhaps of the Holy Father in Rome, whom I despise. The castrati make up the greatest choirs in the Catholic Church. Their manhood is sacrificed to maintain their magical voices in a preadolescent range. There are few things the Church will not do, I realized long ago, to petition the angels in heaven. Dante cannot be more than twenty years old.

"Ciao!" I call as I stride up. *"Che cosa fai?"* What are you doing?

The men hardly look over, they are having so much fun. But the dark-haired woman with the cleft palate eyes me suspiciously. *"Stai zitta!"* she calls. Shut up. "He is a leper. He is to be killed."

"Penso di no." I don't think so. I slowly draw my knife as I move near. "Release him now, and I will spare your lives."

Dante stops singing and the two men with swords now give me their attention. One is a clumsy brute, dark featured, the other, the fair young one, appears quick on his feet. They eye my long narrow knife and chuckle to themselves. But the young man spreads his feet slightly, readying himself for combat. He is an experienced swordsman, although he is not sure yet if I am a boy or a woman. My skin is darker than usual from the sun, the gloss of my red lips partially hidden by my tan. Hanging half upside down, Dante stares at me in wonder, his face a mess of blood and tears. Incredibly, he has hope that I will be able to set him free. Naturally I will, in a few minutes. The brute gestures with his sword.

"Vattene dia," he says. Get away. "Or it will be you we string from the tree."

"It won't happen," I reply, and in a fast move I step forward and cut the top of the woman's left arm. The wound is not serious, it will heal, in time, but I want it to serve as a warning that I am skilled with a blade. Blood springs from her flesh and soaks her peasant clothes. The three hardly saw me move. Yet I know they will need more persuasion than this to back off. Of course I have been here before. A part of me knows that even though it is becoming easier to forget that I have. Surely I will kill them all, for the sake of poor Dante.

The woman screams in pain. "She has cut me! Kill her!"

"You foul creature!" the brute shouts as he dashes forward and tries to run me through. But I have sidestepped his lunge, and tripped him. As he tries to raise his head from the ground, I kneel beside him and pull his head back by the hair. My blade rests across his exposed throat, and I speak to the ugly woman and the fair man, who at least has had the wits to wait to see what I can do.

"If you leave now," I say. "I will let this man live."

"He is no friend of mine," the fair man says. "Do with him what you wish."

"No!" the woman cries. "He is my husband!"

"Then you agree to leave?" I say.

The brute, my knife scratching his trembling throat, is agreeable. "We will be gone," he says.

"Bene." Good. I smash his face in the dirt and then release him. But he is no sooner back on his feet than his dull eyes flash with anger and he makes another try for me. Once again I sidestep the thrust of his sword, but this time I sink my blade deep into his heart and withdraw it before he can take it with him to the bloody ground. His wife cries as he lands facedown. She jumps toward me, her arms flailing, and I kill her as I killed her mate. Now there is only the fair-haired man left. Dante is muttering prayers to

74

heaven and drooling all over his wretched face. Wiping off my knife on the sand, I stand and pull off my cap, letting my blond hair fall. It shines in the last rays of the evening sun. Fair head smiles and nods in appreciation.

"My compliments," he says.

But since he now knows I am a woman, he cannot walk away. Sicilian pride—he finally draws his sword and points it in my direction.

"I have been trained by the Vatican guards," he says. "You may submit to me now, or I will have your head."

Pointing my knife at him, I laugh. "I have been trained by far more experienced teachers. Leave here this instant or I will cut you badly."

He takes a step closer. "My name is Pino. I would take no pleasure in killing such a beautiful woman as you. Drop your knife, and let us take pleasure in each other."

"No," I say. "I would rather kill you."

He moves closer still. The tip of his blade dangles three feet from my face—I could almost reach out, without moving my feet, and take it from him. But I am too much the good sport, and I don't want Dante to see me as a supernatural being. Then I might have to kill him as well. It is funny, how I know Dante, without even being introduced to him.

"You are young," Pino says. "Why make such a rash decision?"

"You are proud," I say. "You have seen my skills. Why not withdraw? Your death will prove nothing here."

He smiles but I have angered him. He takes a swipe

at me with his blade, trying to cut my left shoulder. But he misses, and another smooth swipe also fails to draw blood. He appears more puzzled than worried.

"You move well," he says.

"Last chance," I say. "Leave or die."

"All right, cold woman," he says as he turns to leave. "I am no match for you." But he has hardly turned his back on me when he spins and tries to take off my head with his sword. Ducking, I thrust forward and plant my blade in his abdomen. There I leave it as I back off a few steps. He is still regaining his balance from his failed attack. He stares down at my knife in amazement. I don't know if he understands yet that his wound is fatal.

"What have you done?" he gasps as blood begins to show around my knife. Dropping his sword, he reaches down and pulls out the knife with both hands. Bad move—now the blood spurts out, over his hands and onto the ground. He still cannot comprehend that I have defeated him. "You witch!"

"I am not a witch," I say casually. "I am a good Samaritan. This man you torture has done nothing to hurt you."

Pino drops to his knees, bleeding over everything. "But he is a leper," he gasps.

"That is better than a corpse." I come closer so that I stand above him. I stick out my hand. "May I have my knife back please?"

He stares at me, incredulous. But he hands me back my knife, as if I might now help him because he is cooperating. But he is beyond a cure. I take a step toward Dante, whose head bobbles like that of a puppy dog.

"Oh, my lady," he gushes. "God has sent you."

I begin to cut him down. "Somebody did," I say.

Pino cries out to me as he slumps to the ground. There is great sorrow in his words, but I have heard it all before over the centuries. *"Non voglio morire."* I don't want to die.

Dante answers for me, giving me a future favorite line.

"Then you should never have been born," he says.

8

Later, at night around a fire, I muse to myself that I killed the two men and the woman exactly as I had killed them before. The knowledge that their deaths were certain did not affect my actions in the slightest. Not even a single word that was exchanged between us was different. It makes me wonder whose future I'm from.

Dante sits across from me, wrapped in the swordsman's finery. He has washed out Pino's blood. My new friend is busy gloating over a rabbit I caught for him. A stick skewered through it, the meat hangs in the fire growing more tasty by the minute. The dripping grease crackles in the flames. Dante licks his diseased fingers and his dark eyes shine with joy. He has been muttering prayers to himself since I saved him.

"Tis a wonderful eve, I know," he says. "The light of heaven follows our steps. There can be no other way of explaining how a helpless maid was able to rescue me."

I laugh. "Dante, please don't call me that. Or I will show you again just how wrong you are."

He is instantly apologetic. "I meant no offense, my lady. I intended only to praise the grace of God. You are his instrument in this world, I know that in my heart." He adjusts the rabbit in the fire and licks his cracked lips. "We can eat soon."

"You can have it all," I say. "I have already eaten today."

He is offended. "If you will not feed with me, my lady, I myself will go hungry. It is not right that I should keep taking from you."

I continue to smile. "There is one thing you can give me—information. I have never been in Sicily before. Tell me about this land?"

He brightens. "It is a beautiful land, my lady, filled with sweet orchards and tall trees that cover the hills. You stay around Messina and wander not too far from the well-traveled roads, and you will have a pleasant visit."

"If I had not been far off the well-traveled roads this evening, I would not have been there to rescue you. But I am curious why you say I should stay close to Messina. Surely the Moslems have not landed on Sicily's southern shores?"

His face darkens. "But they have, my lady. A force of them is camped on the beaches in the southwest. Have you not heard?"

"No. I heard that the Duke of Terra di Labur is strong in the south, with many armed knights."

Dante trembles. "Do not speak that name, my lady, for he no longer goes by it. He has turned against the Christian God, and has murdered his own knights. It is by his power and with his protection that the heathens have managed to land their forces on Sicily."

I am surprised, even though I know all these things deep inside. Yet the future becomes more a dream to me with each passing hour. I know it exists, I know I am from there, but I have to focus to maintain this knowledge. Yet this does not worry me. It seems entirely natural that I should be one hundred percent in the present moment, with Dante, and the cooking rabbit, and his stories of the evil duke. But I have spoiled Dante's appetite by asking about the latter. Dante stares miserably at the fire as if he were staring at a picture of hell. He scratches at his lepered arm and leg—my questions bring him pain. Yet I know I must ask all about the political details.

"What does the duke call himself now?" I ask.

Dante shakes his head. "It is better not to repeat it in the night lest he hear us talking of him. For the night is his cloak, and shadows flow around him."

I laugh again. "Come on, he can't be that bad. I must know his name."

Dante is adamant. "I am sorry, my lady, I will not talk of him. To do so is a sin to your good company."

"My good company will not be so good if you do not answer me. What is the Duke's name now?"

Dante speaks in a whisper. "Landulf of Capua."

I have heard the name before, of course. But now it rings in my ears with less potency and more harmless connotations. Myth surrounds the title, not remembered agonies. Yet I know Landulf is the one I have come for—from the stars, for the stars—even if the flames that sparkle before my eyes blot out most of the nighttime sky. I do not want to focus on future facts—it is another choice I make. I am more intrigued than scared. Capua is tied to Landulf's name because he was originally from there.

"I know this name," I say. "Even in Italy, the farmers in the countryside speak of him. They say he is an evil wizard, capable of performing magical acts." I pause. "Dante, why are you crying?"

He is really devastated. "It is nothing, my lady. Let us talk of another person." He pokes at the rabbit with another stick he has found. "Or we can just eat, you can have some meat. You must be hungry after such a long day."

There is something in his tone that catches my attention. "Do you personally know this Landulf of Capua?" I ask.

He stiffens. "No."

"You must know him to be so frightened of him."

He rubs at his leper arm. Actually, the disease has spread so far, he has only a stump left. His left leg is also little more than a stump; he walks with the aid of a wooden brace I found not far from where he was strung up. His sores are open and fluid oozes from them. He must be near death, yet he has energy. But now his strength is in a whirlwind of constant motion. His eyes are moist and he cannot stop shaking.

"I cannot talk about him," he begs. "Please do not force me to say his name."

"Dante," I say. "Look at me."

He raises his head. "My lady?"

"Stare deep into my eyes, my dear friend," I say

81

gently, carefully bending his will to mine. "You need not be afraid to speak of this duke. He cannot harm you now."

Dante blinks and his tears begin to dry. "He cannot harm me," he whispers.

"That is true," I say. "Now tell me about him, how you came to know him."

Dante sits back and stares at the fire again. He has forgotten the rabbit. He is half in a trance, half in a dream. I know I am asking him to repeat a nightmarish section of life. For even though I have calmed him with my power, his withered leg and arm continue to twitch. It is almost as if his leprosy was given to him by the duke, but that I find hard to believe.

Yet I do believe it. I *know* it.

What do I know? The stars are far away.

Dante's face holds my attention.

"My duke was not merely a duke, but an archbishop and a special friend of the Holy Father," Dante says, in a clearer voice than usual. "It was to Rome my duke brought me at the age of ten to serve as his personal attendant and to sing in the Vatican choir. The Holy Father said my voice was a sacrament, and I was allowed to join the privileged castrati and sacrifice my manhood to the Church. This I did not mind, as long as I was allowed to stay close to my duke. For five years I was at peace within the holy walls, and I thought of nothing but my duty and my vows." He pauses and sighs. Even though he is partly hypnotized, his pain comes through. "Then, it happened, one terrible day, that my duke was falsely accused."

"What was he accused of?"

Dante hesitates. "I thought it was a lie."

"Did the pope accuse him?"

"Yes. The Holy Father himself."

"Of what?" I repeat.

Dante pauses before he answers. "Of invoking the spirit of Satan."

I do not believe in such nonsense, nevertheless, his words are chilling. "Was he cast out?" I ask.

Dante coughs. The smoke of the burning logs has entered his lungs. The agony of remembering suffocates him, too. "There was a trial," he says. "The cardinals and the Holy Father were present. Accusations were made, then witnesses were called—I had never seen these people before. Each one came forth and stated how my beloved duke had poisoned their minds with demonic spirits. Even I was called to denounce him. The Holy Father made me swear to tell the truth and then—in the same breath—told me to tell lies." A tear rolls over Dante's ruined face. "I did not know what to say. But I had never seen my duke commit any of these sins. I was afraid but I knew in my heart I could not lie." A hysterical note enters his voice. "Jesus never lied, even when he stood before his accusers."

"Be calm, Dante," I say soothingly. "That was long ago. None of it can hurt you now. Just tell me what happened."

He relaxes some, but shifts closer to the fire, as if chilled.

"The pope grew angry at me, and accused me of being in league with Satan and my duke. I was chained to my seat and more witnesses were called, more people I had never seen before. These spoke against me as well as my duke, while the cardinals whispered among themselves. I was very afraid. They were talking about burning us. I did not know what to do!"

"Peace, Dante, peace. Continue."

Dante swallows thickly before continuing. On top of everything else, he seems to have trouble breathing. A frown wrinkles his features and he blinks, trying to remember where he is, or where he has been. Yet his voice remains clear.

"We were led away, my duke and I, and thrown into a stone cell where criminals were normally taken. We spent the night together in that stinking place. My fear was great—I knew we were about to be killed. But my duke acted pleased. He said nothing could harm us, that the Holy Father would be forced to release us."

"Were you released?" I ask. My knowledge of the inner workings of the Vatican is extensive. No one accused by the pope of consorting with Satan ever survives. Such mercy would set a poor precedent. Yet Dante nods in response to my question.

"The next morning the jailer came and opened our door. There stood the Holy Father. He said the judgment of the holy council was that we were to be let go, but to be banned from the city of Rome. My duke's titles and properties were not confiscated, and I was amazed. My duke knelt and kissed the pope's ring before we were led away, and then he stared into the pope's eyes, and for the first time I saw the Holy Father afraid." Dante pauses. "I was afraid as well."

"Of your duke?"

"Yes."

"Why?"

He gestures with a stump. "Because it was as if a black snake reached out from his eyes and touched the Holy Father between the eyes. A snake the others could not see."

"But you saw it?" I ask

"Yes."

"How?"

He speaks with conviction. "It was there!"

"I understand." I have to calm him again, not allow him to come out of his trance. "What did you and your duke do next?"

"Traveled to Persida."

The name is not familiar. "Where is that?"

"Not far."

"Where?"

"Near. Hidden."

I find it strange he is able to avoid answering me directly, and wonder if powerful hypnotic powers have already been brought to bear on his memory.

"What is special about Persida?" I ask carefully.

He coughs painfully. "It is where magic was first invented."

"By your duke?"

"Yes."

"Why did you stay with him in Persida?"

Dante struggles. "I had to."

"Why?" I insist. "Did he use magic on you?"

He bursts with memories. "Yes! He called forth the great serpent! The living Satan! He invoked it in pain and blood and it poured forth from his navel. I saw it again, the snake—it grew from his intestines and screeched when it saw the light of the world. He poisoned my soul with its filthy powers, and then he poisoned my body."

"That's when you started to get sick?"

He calms down, so sad. "Yes. In Persida, where magic lived, I began to die."

"Why did he make you sick?"

"For his pleasure."

"But you were a loyal subject?"

More tears. "He did not care. It pleased him to see me eaten away."

I want him to go on. "What did he do next?"

"He went to Kalot Enbolot. That is the door to Sicily. He has a castle there. It was given to him by the Holy Father. He wanted to open the door to the heathens."

"To let the Moslems overrun the Christian world through Sicily?"

"Yes."

"And it was there he took up the name Landulf?"

"Lord Landulf of Capua."

"How did he slay his knights? At the castle?"

"He made them slay one another. The demons summoned by the sacrifices always demand betrayal."

"You keep saying he invoked demons, that he summoned them. What proof do you have of this other than the snakes you thought you saw?"

"I did see them!"

"Fine. But what was Landulf able to do with these demons?"

"He used them to torture men. To control their wills." Dante stops and glances away from the fire, into the dark, and his whole body shakes. "Distance does not matter with these demons. They can cross water and bring death. In the fair land of England, my duke boasted, knights in search of the Holy Grail wander lost because of the spells he cast over them. They will never find the Grail, he said. Forever, they will be lost."

I was familiar with this mystical quest. But it was

hard for me to imagine that Landulf had a hand in it. "Why does he bother with these knights?" I ask.

Dante speaks with pride. "Because they are righteous, and the light of God shines before them."

"But you say Landulf is stronger than they are?"

Dante hangs his head, as if ashamed. "I am afraid that he is the strongest."

"But you are a Christian. Your Lord Jesus Christ says no demon can stand before the name of Christ."

Dante continues, dejected, "Landulf cannot be defeated."

"Surely he is not all powerful. You escaped from him. How did you manage to do that?"

But Dante shakes his head. "I did not escape. He sent me away."

"Why?"

Dante looks me straight in the eye, and I believe my power has finally failed. He is no longer in a trance, but he is still frightened, more so than ever—terrified of what he has already told me, what I may do with the knowledge.

"My lady, he told me to find him an immortal ruby beyond all worth. And bring her back to him."

An immortal ruby? My vampiric blood?

It sounds as if Landulf of Capua already knows about me.

That is fair. I intend to know a lot more about him.

I will go to his castle, I decide.

Dante will lead me to the black wizard.

9

It takes a week to walk to Landulf's aerie, which stands in the heights of Monte Castello, in southwest Sicily, where, Dante tells me, the Oracle of Venus, the Goddess of Love, once stood. Dante knows a tremendous amount of Roman and Greek history and mythology. He is much more educated than I would have guessed. I begin to understand that one of the reasons Landulf kept him around was because of his powerful story-telling abilities. Even the evil duke loved a good tale, and when Dante starts on a story, his whole demeanor changes, as if he were hypnotized, and he speaks with great eloquence. But the moment the tale is over, he reverts. The sudden personality changes are disconcerting, but I am sympathetic to him because he has obviously been warped by his exposure to Landulf. I feel guilty that I am manipulating him further. Only by dominating him with my eyes, by soothing him several times a day, am I able to persuade him to lead the way to the castle. The thought of the place fills him with dread and he must be wondering that his legs continue to carry him in that direction.

Yet he doesn't seem to wonder about me. His affection for me is genuine; it pains me to use him so. And it is obvious that he is more concerned about me than about himself. When my influence on him wanes, he begs me to turn back. The human sacrifices he tells me about as being commonplace at the castle fill me with doubt. It is hard to believe there could exist such evil as he describes. Of course that is Dante's point. Landulf is no longer human. He has become a beast he invoked. The devil lives and breathes on a peak once considered sacred in ancient Rome. Before resting each night, Dante recites the entire mass in Latin, praying to a small copper cross he hides during the day in the wooden brace that supports his leper's stump. At night I see him scratching at his sores, and his suffering weighs on my heart. Only a devil, I think, could have cursed him so.

Yet I still do not believe in his Christian demons.

But what draws me to meet Landulf is the chance to witness his magic, whether it be white or black. Although I know for a fact it will be black, that I have visited the cruel wizard already. But what I remember of the future grows more abstract with each passing day. The dirt paths of old Sicily are my only guides. I remember Alanda's name but I cannot imagine her face. At night, though, I stare for hours at the stars, trying to convince myself that I was once there, in a mysterious ship, with creatures from another world.

And perhaps with the gods of ancient myths.

Dante wants to tell me about Perseus as we walk.

I am familiar with the mythology, of course, having lived in ancient Greece for many years. But Dante insists I have not heard it properly, and it seems to be one of his favorite stories, so I let him speak. But talking as he walks is a luxury Dante can ill afford. Often he must stop to lean on me for support, but now he is remarkably energetic. He has found a stout walking stick that helps him walk as he speaks with loving enthusiasm about the ancient hero. Obviously Dante worships such characters, and wishes he were one, instead of the crippled leper he is. A handsome young god who could sweep away a beautiful princess such as me. I know Dante is more than a little in love with me.

"Perseus was the son of Zeus and Danaë. His grandfather was Acrisius, a cruel king, who visited the oracle at Delphi and learned that his daughter's child was destined to be the instrument of his death. Perseus and his mother were therefore locked in a chest and set adrift on the ocean. The chest floated to Seriphus, where it was found by a fisherman and brought to the king of the land, Polydectes, a generous man who received them with love. When Perseus had become a young man, Polydectes sent him to destroy the Medusa, a terrible monster that was laying waste to his land and turning men to stone. History has it that Medusa had once been a beautiful maiden whose hair was her chief glory. But she dared to compare herself to Athena, and in revenge the goddess changed her wonderful curls into hissing snakes and she became a monster," Dante pauses. "But that's not what happened."

I have to smile It is only a story.

"What *really* happened, my friend?" I ask, a mocking note in my voice.

Dante is not dissuaded. "The Medusa never compared herself to anyone. She thought she was beyond comparison, beyond all the gods and goddesses. It was only her hair that became monstrous—her face remained beautiful."

I laugh. "That is good to know."

"It is an important point. One never knows if it was her beauty or the serpents on her head that were able to turn men and other creatures to stone. But I must continue with the tale. Perseus, given a divine shield by Athena, and winged shoes by Hermes, approached Medusa's cave while the monster slept. Perseus took special care not to look directly at her. All around him in the cavern were the stone figures of men and women and animals who had chanced to gaze at the evil creature. Guided only by the Medusa's image reflected in his bright shield, he cut off her head and ended the threat of the monster."

"Then he gave the head to Athena?" I knew the end, I thought. Dante shook his head and spoke seriously.

"That is not true. He kept it for himself. It was with the Medusa's head that he was able to defeat Atlas, and steal the gods' golden apples. It was only with the Medusa's head that he was able to turn to stone the Titan that was threatening to eat Andromeda, who would later become his wife." Dante shook his head again. "Perseus never gave up the severed head of the Gorgon. It was too valuable a weapon."

I continue to smile, even though I know we draw

close to Landulf's castle. The forest has changed, become wilder and darker, filled with trees that have twisted arms for branches, sharp nails for leaves. A gloom hangs over the land and it depresses even me, me who is usually not affected by subtle elemental vibrations. Even the sun's rays are dimmed by a gray overcast that appears made more of dust than water vapor. There is a constant odor of smoke, and I believe I detect the stench of burnt bodies. Still, I think I am an invincible vampire, no easy victim for Landulf and his black sorcery.

"That is only one version of the story," I say.

Dante regards me with disappointment.

"It is the correct version, my lady," he says. "It is an important story. Hidden within it are many great truths."

"You will have to explain them to me another time." I pause and survey the land ahead. We are in rugged mountains made of hard rock and dry river-beds. In the distance hangs a black mist that even my supernatural vision cannot pierce. This unnatural cloud clings to some kind of massive stone structure, but I cannot discern the details. I point and ask, "What is that?"

Dante is suddenly the cowering fool again. He clings to my arm and the fluid from his open sores stains my white shirt. "It is our death, my lady. There is still time to turn back. Before his thralls come for us in the black of night."

"Who are his thralls?"

Dante speaks in a frightened whisper. "Men who have no hearts, and yet still live. I swear to you I have seen these creatures. They see without eyes and have no need to breathe fresh air."

"How many men does Landulf have at his command?"

Dante is animated. "You don't understand, my lady. His power is not in strength of arms. Had he not one man, he could still hold off the full might of Rome, and the Moslems for that matter. Even they fear him."

I grip Dante's shoulders. "Tell me how many men he has under his command. Even an estimate will help me."

Dante is having trouble catching his breath. "I never counted them. It must be several hundred."

"Two hundred? Eight hundred?"

Dante coughs. "Maybe five hundred. But they are not important. It is the spirits that haunt this land that will kill us. They are in the trees, the rocks—he sends them out to spy on those who dare to challenge him. He must already know we are here. We have to go back!"

I am gentle, but I do hold his eye. "Dante, my friend, you have done me a great service. I know you didn't want to come here but you have. And I know it was out of love and respect for me. But now you have repaid your debt to me. You are free to return the way you have come. I want you to return to Messina, and save yourself. There is no need for you to go any farther along this road."

To my surprise, my power over him is outweighed by his love for me. He shakes his head and pleads with me. "You do not know what he will do to you. He has powers you cannot imagine. A lust for cruelty and pain that cannot be spoken. He rips the eyes from his victims and stores them in jars to later feed to caged rats he keeps in his personal quarters. He pulls the bones from slaves before their very eyes and munches on them at gruesome suppers. All this he does to set the stage for his satanic invocations. But when the spirits come, there is nowhere to hide." Dante weeps and grips my arm fiercely. "Please don't go there, my lady! In God's holy name I beg you!"

I kiss him, stroke his face, and then shake my head.

"I must go," I say. "But I will go in the name of your God, if it comforts you, and the name of my God as well. Wish me luck, my dear Dante, and take care of yourself. You are a precious soul, and I have known so few in my life."

He is in despair. "My lady?"

"Goodbye. Do not worry about me."

I turn and walk deeper into the gloom.

I do not hear him follow.

Yet all around me darkness deepens.

The sun still shines.

10 ❧

This castle and its enclosure are built at the top of a cliff. Coming within a mile, I am able to see through the mist enough to know that the rear of the castle is unapproachable. The drop down the back is virtually straight, a thousand feet easily. Unable to see beyond the drop, I know that the ocean must lie not far beyond that—two miles at most. With such a commanding view of the sea and coast, Landulf would be able to spot enemies approaching at any point along southern Sicily. His home is strategically placed—as Dante said—as a doorway to the Christian world.

Outside the castle proper but still within the high stone wall are many small houses, some for living, others military structures where horses and arms are stored. Soldiers with swords wander around small fires, cooking meat, talking among themselves. Over them hangs the bulk of the castle—much larger than I had imagined it. These fires, I see, could not be responsible for the strange mist. Yet I no longer smell cooking human flesh and have to wonder if I imagined it.

I glance behind me. The shadows have grown long, the day is almost over. Dante is nowhere in sight. Yet I hear horses approaching from behind me, where I left Dante. They have a cart of some kind—its wheels creak on the rutted path. Above, a thick branch hangs over me and in a single leap I am cloaked within the leaves of the tree. The castle will have to wait for a moment. I want to see what these men are up to.

Minutes later I receive partial verification of Dante's wild tales.

On the cart is a cage, with metal bars. Three desperate females are locked inside. They are naked, but the four soldiers who have captured them are in full battle gear. Two drive the horses, while the other two are on horseback, one at the front, the other at the rear. The men are young but appear strong and battle tested. The females are each about eighteen. There is, of course, no way I can allow them to be taken into Landulf's castle, even if my intervening might upset my plans.

Vaguely, I remember I have rescued them before.

My plan of attack is simple.

As the first horse passes beneath me, a hundred feet in front of the cage, I drop down and land on the animal right behind the soldier. He is surprised to have company. I don't give him a chance to experience the wonder. Reaching up, I grab the back of his head and twist his skull. There is an explosion of bone and cartilage in his neck. He sags to the side, dead, and I shove him from the horse. Behind me, the two horses pulling the cage rear up. My horse I bring to a halt, and turn to face the others.

Already my long knife is out. Whipping my arm through a blinding arc, I let go of the hilt and plant the blade in the forehead of one of the drivers. The other driver draws his sword. I am forced to run toward him empty-handed. But I receive unexpected help from one of the females. As the soldier raises his sword to strike me, a girl with long hair gives him a swift kick in the back. He loses his balance and topples toward me. Before he hits the ground I relieve him of his sword and cut off his head.

There is still the fourth soldier, the one bringing up the rear. He has drawn a bow and arrow and is taking aim at me. He is an excellent shot. In the blink of an eye I see an arrow fly toward my head. Ducking, I realize that even though it will miss me, it will strike one of the girls. I am reluctant to show too many of my powers, but I have no choice. As the arrow flies by, I reach up and grab it and then break it over my knee.

The fourth soldier is worried.

"I am going to release the women," I say to him, staring. "They will ride back the way they have come."

The soldier just nods.

There are keys to the cage tied to the belt of the soldier who has my knife in his forehead. I relieve him of these and open the cage, marveling at the intricacy of the lock. The craftsmanship is far beyond anything I have seen before. But the keys work fine and a moment later the women are free. I give the reins to the one who assisted me, and throw the cloak from a dead soldier over her.

"Ride fast from here," I say catching her eye. "Do not speak to anyone about me."

She nods. I step from the cart as she turns it around. In seconds the women in the cart are out of sight. Slowly I walk toward the remaining soldier, who has moved aside to let the women pass. I admire his courage, that he has not tried to bolt. But he is still a kidnapper, and I am thirsty. The soldier draws his sword as I approach but I shake my head.

"You are going to die," I say. "It is better not to resist."

He swings at my head, misses. Stepping forward, I grab the hand that holds his sword and look up into his frightened eyes. "Who sent you to capture those women?" I ask. "Was it Landulf?"

He shakes his head. "No."

"Who then?"

He refuses to answer me, even though I press him with my eyes. He continues to shake his head, and I am puzzled. I finally pull him from his horse and throw his sword aside. Drawing his face near, I let him feel the warmth of my breath.

"What is he like?" I ask.

The man is resolute. "He is my lord and my master."

"Is he evil?"

He sneers. "You are evil!"

I have to laugh. "I suppose I am—to you."

He dies, in my arms, from blood loss. Afterward, I feel refreshed, ready for more action. The bodies I hide in the bushes beside the path. The blood, even, I cover over with mud. I wash and dress like a young boy again, my hair under my cap. Then I walk toward the castle and boldly knock at the iron gate that guards the entrance in the wall. A host of soldiers answer and I am stern with them.

"I am here to see Landulf of Capua," I say in a powerful voice. "Bring me to him."

They lead me through the courtyard filled with soldiers and smoke to the castle door. A servant comes, and then another. They all seem fairly normal, although I obviously make them nervous. Finally the woman of the house arrives, Landulf's wife, Lady Cia. A striking woman, she wears a high-necked, tight-sleeved, long tunic belted at the waist. Many jewels adorn her hair and elegant fingers. Her hair is black and worn up and her eyes are dark. She is not Mediterranean but English. Her smile is welcoming, yet it doesn't reach her eyes. She is exceedingly thin, and holds herself under rigid control. I cannot say I warm to her, but she is anything but threatening. Certainly she does not seem afraid of me. I have left my long knife with the bodies of the soldiers.

Lady Cia invites me in without many questions. I don't ask why a man who used to be an archbishop now has a wife. Since the pope doesn't want him, I think, he may have decided to enjoy good company.

"It is seldom we get visitors from Greece," she says, when I explain where I have just come from. "But that is not your home, is it, Sita?"

Removing my cap, I shake out my blond hair. "No. Like you, I am from England."

She is pleased. "You are perceptive. But surely you are not traveling through the country by yourself?"

I act sad. "No. I was with my uncle. But there was an accident on the road, and he was killed."

She touches her heart. "I am so sorry. What was the accident?"

"His horse threw him. His neck broke."

She shakes her head and leads me deeper into the castle. "You poor dear. You must be devastated. Let us give you food, shelter."

"Thank you."

The castle is magnificent, and although my eyes strain to detect anything odd, the only unusual thing I see is an excess of wealth, even for a Sicilian aerie commanded by a duke. Landulf has sculptures from all along the Mediterranean. The marble on his floor is inlaid with gold, and the plaster ceilings are warmed by wooden beams. Everything is tasteful, not an offense to the eye. I compliment Cia on her home.

"My husband prides himself on his collections." She points to a marble statue from ancient Greece. "Since you were just in that part of the world, I am sure you would appreciate our hero."

I approach the statue, touch it, think of Dante, and pray he is all right. Perseus holds the head of the Medusa in one upraised hand, a sword in the other. His head is slightly bowed; his great exploit has not made him proud. But the face of the Gorgon is a horror; even in death she finds no peace. A feeling of disquiet sweeps over me, but I push it away. I have seen this statue before, of course I have. Lady Cia stands by my side.

"Can I have a servant show you to your room?" she asks. "You can rest and wash. Then perhaps you can join us for supper."

"You and Lord Landulf?"

She does not flinch at the name. "Yes. We would both enjoy the company." She snaps a finger and a chubby maid appears. "Marie will show you to your room."

I grasp her hands. They are cold, although the castle is warm, with fires burning in most corners. She trembles at my touch but I steady her with my strength. Staring deep into her eyes, I notice nothing supernatural.

"You are most kind," I say.

Marie leads me up three flights of stairs before we come to my quarters. Along the way we pass a window covered with iron bars, and I see that night has firmly arrived. Marie is dressed in a long black tunic over a white chemise. With a rosary around her neck, she could have been a nun. A few of Landulf's walls are covered with frescoes, paintings done directly on fresh plaster. Most of these have a spiritual theme. He seems to have an obsession with the Old Testament. The God that looks over his household is often angry.

Marie opens a door onto a small room. There is linen on the straw mattress and a bowl of water. Marie lights a row of candles and asks if I need anything else.

"No thank you," I say.

She leaves and I am alone. Washing my hands in the water provided, I am at a loss to explain why I keep looking around for a faucet with running water. Then I remember there are such niceties, in other places. The water is cold but seems fresh. I drink some and it rinses away the blood in my mouth. I do not understand how the soldier was able to resist my questions.

11 ~

A short time later I am at Lord Landulf's supper table. An old spear is fastened to the wall. It is this spear that the room seems to be designed around. From the massive stone fireplace logs crack and shoot showers of sparks out into the room as I am introduced to Lord Landulf by Lady Cia.

"This is the young woman I told you about," she says. "She came to our door not more than an hour ago, seeking asylum. Her traveling companion, her uncle, has just been killed on the road. Sita, this is the duke and my husband, Lord Landulf."

He is not a tall man and looks frail, which surprises me, after all the gruesome stories I have heard of him. Yet his delicateness is not necessarily a sign of weakness. He appears to be physically agile, and I suspect he is an accomplished swordsman. He wears a neatly trimmed black mustache and a pointed graying beard. He has oily smooth skin, and is dressed impeccably in a dark red silk chemise with long, tight sleeves, black hose, and a red and gold embroidery tunic, which comes down past his knees. His hands, like those of his wife, are decorated with many uncut gems and pearls. A ruby on his left middle finger is the largest I have ever seen. His voice, when he speaks is cultured, educated and refined. His large dark eyes are warm but shrewd. He clicks his soft, heelless leather shoes together and bows in my direction.

"Lady Sita," he says. "It is a pleasure."

I offer my hand. "The pleasure is mine, Lord Landulf."

He kisses my middle finger, and glances up at me. "Surprise visitors are always the most enchanting."

"Hidden castles are always the most exciting," I say with a smile.

We sit down to a vegetable soup. Lady Cia leads us in a brief prayer. There are only us three at the table; we have four servants waiting on us. The soup is finished when Landulf inquires about my travels. Considering the expansion of the Arab World, it is impossible to talk for more than a few minutes without the subject turning to the invading Moslems. At this Landulf's mood turns foul.

"Six of those heathen ships tried to land on a beach not five miles from here," he says bitterly. "They came in on a wave of fog, but my scouts were wary. We were able to set fire to their sails before they reached land. All their people were lost in the tides."

His remark stuns me. "You fight the Moslems here?" I ask.

"Of course," he says, and there is a gleam in his eye as he studies me. "Have you heard different?"

I lower my head. "No, my lord."

"Come," he says with force, "we are sharing food. Why have secrets between friends? You have obviously traveled far and wide with your uncle. You know more of Greece than I do. What have you heard of my relationship with the Moslems?"

I hesitate, then decide I may as well dive in. "The word is that you are in league with them."

He does not lose his temper as I fear. But the air chills. "It is only in Rome they would speak such lies," he says.

"I have been in Rome," I say. "Not three months ago."

"Oh dear," Lady Cia mutters anxiously. "We did not know you had been exposed to such matters."

Landulf raises his hand. "It doesn't matter. In the short time I have known Sita, it is obvious to me she is not taken in by every story shared by every frustrated priest and nun."

"That is true, my lord," I say.

Landulf pulls his chair back from the table and sighs. "It is true that the Holy Father and I have gone our separate ways. But our differences were and still are more political than spiritual. Nicholas believes we should fortify our defenses, and wait for the Moslems to break against our walls. But I know this foe too well. I have met these bloodthirsty monsters on the battlefield. If we do not attack, push the war back into their own lands, they will see us as weak and never leave us in peace." Landulf stands and steps away from the table. "But all that is a question of strategy, and in my own land I pursue my own counsel. But to hear the talk in Rome I have denounced the Church and turned against Christ himself." He pauses. "Is that what you have heard, Lady Sita?"

I have already taken the plunge. The wild tales I may as well validate, or else put aside. "I have heard worse, my lord," I say. "The peasants say you conjure evil forces. That you are a master of the black arts and able to raise demons from the depths of hell."

Landulf is momentarily struck, then laughs long and hard. His wife joins him after a tense moment. "I would like to meet one of these peasants and ask him where he gets his information!" he exclaims. "That is the trouble with lies. They are perpetually pregnant. At every turn they give birth to more lies."

"There was a peasant I met along the roads," I say carefully. "He acted as if he knew you. His name was Dante. You've heard of him?"

Lady Cia gushes. "Dante? My lord has known him since he was a child. Pray tell us where you met him?"

I am evasive. "When I was lost in the woods, after my uncle died. But that was three days' journey from here." I add, "Dante seemed lost as well, and I shared food with him."

"I pray you did not share anything else with him," Landulf says darkly, referring to Dante's leprosy.

"I was careful always to keep a safe distance," I say. "But when he spoke of this place, it was with fear. I couldn't understand why."

"Surely you must know," Lady Cia says. "It is his illness. Since he became ill, he has spoken of nothing but demons that chase after his soul."

Again Lord Landulf raises his hand. "It is not so easy as that. I am partly to blame for his condition. When I brought him to Rome, as a boy, the Holy

Father became enamored of his singing voice. Without my consent or knowledge, the pope had him castrated, so that his voice would remain high. Dante took the loss of his manhood badly, and I think he never ceased blaming me for the disfigurement. Since I was the cause of one physical aberration, when the illness came over him, he blamed me for that as well."

"But we tried to keep Dante here, and comfortable," Lady Cia says. "It was just that our servants feared his illness and he himself felt he needed to be free to roam the world."

Landulf shakes his head. "It pains me to know that my own friend has joined the chorus against me. Very well, leadership has its price. I cannot turn from the task I have set before me, to protect the underbelly of the Christian world. If I go to my grave cursed by every cardinal in the Vatican, at least I will still be able to hold my head up high when I meet my Lord in heaven."

"That is all that matters," I mutter.

Landulf steps closer to the fire, to the spear, and points out the aged iron tip to me. "Sita, do you know what this is?"

I stand and join him near the object. There is a single crude nail bound to the spear by circles of wire. The black shaft, I see, has more recently been joined to the tip—it is not nearly so old. Landulf touches the metal spear tip lovingly, running his fingers over the tapered edges, which are surprisingly sharp given the spear's obvious antiquity.

"I have never seen it before," I say.

He nods. "Few people have, except those who have been chosen to lead the fight against unrighteousness.

This is the Spear of Longinus, sometimes called the Maurice Spear. It is this very spear that Gaius Cassius, a Roman Centurion under the command of Pro-Consul Pontius Pilate, used to pierce the side of the blessed Lord himself. Thus he put an end to Jesus' suffering on the cross. The final prophecy from the Old Testament that Jesus had to fulfill to prove that he was the true Messiah was that of Isaiah, who said, 'A bone of Him not be broken.' You see, Sita, at the time Jesus suffered on the cross, Annas and Caiaphas, high priests of the Sanhedrin, were trying to convince the Romans to kill Jesus before the Sabbath began. It was the priests' hope that the Romans would mutilate Jesus' body, and therefore prove that he was not the chosen one. But Gaius Cassius, although a Roman soldier, was devoted to Jesus and his teachings, and did not want to see Jesus' body defiled. He took up this spear of his own free will, and in that moment all the prophecies of the world were held in balance in his hand. But at the moment this spear pierced Jesus' side, all the prophecies were fulfilled. For that reason, it is said that whoever holds this spear commands the destiny of the world." Landulf paused and smiled slightly. "It is the story that is told about it."

And a fascinating one, too. I reach out and touch the spear, and feel a strange power sweep over me. It is unlike anything I have ever experienced before, at least none that I can remember. But vaguely the thought of a brown-skinned child comes to my mind. The spear is a weapon of war, yet somehow it comforts me. I touch the tip and think of the blood that once spilled over it. The blood that supposedly had the power to wash away all sins. Standing beside

Landulf, I feel the weight of all the people I have murdered for their blood. He seems to sense something odd because he stares at me intensely.

"Sita?" he says.

"But you believe this story?" I say in an unsteady voice.

He continues to watch me. "I do, but then I am a romantic at heart." He leans close and whispers in my ear. "What do you feel when you touch it, Sita?"

I momentarily close my eyes. "I feel the child," I whisper.

"The baby Jesus?"

"John."

He moves back. "The Baptist?"

I open my eyes, confused. For an instant the face of Suzama flashes in my mind. But she had no children, I think. Suzama was celibate. Yet the name of John haunts me, as does the face of a child I cannot quite pinpoint.

"I was not thinking of the Baptist," I say.

"What then?" he insists.

In that moment, in that castle, I cannot remember.

"I don't know," I say.

He gestures to the table. "Why don't we finish our meal?"

"Thank you."

He takes me by the hand and leads me back to the meal.

12 〜

Later, in my room, I feel dull and tired. I am four thousand years old, I do not normally need much sleep. Yet my vision is now blurred with fatigue. Staring in a mirror surrounded by candles, I feel as if my face changes into that of a person from another time and my blond hair turns dark red. The candles grow to the size of the flames that burned in the fireplace. Splashing water on my face, I feel some of the illusions leave me, but they do not go away. There is an unpleasant taste in my mouth that the water cannot wash away.

Then it strikes me.

I have been drugged.

Landulf, perhaps with his wife's knowledge, had something put in my food. There is no other explanation for my lethargy. But it is unlikely that the drug was administered for my benefit—a good night's sleep in a castle rumored to be filled with demons. If he has drugged me it is because he wants me unconscious so that he can do something awful to me. All of Dante's tales come back to me in a haunting wave, and I am amazed at how I have dropped my guard. But could my carelessness have something to do with Landulf's magic?

For all I know, his drug was poison and I am already doomed.

I force myself to vomit. Then I drink the water left in the bowl and vomit again. Within seconds my head clears, but I am still far from being at full strength. Moving to the door, I find it locked by a device as sophisticated as the one I found on the cage that held the young women. The metal parts are made of a peculiar alloy—stronger than anything I have ever encountered. Fortunately the door, although thick oak, is only wood. Leaning hard on it, and taking deep breaths to clear my system of the lingering effects of the drug, I am able to break it open without much noise.

Marie stands outside my door.

I grab her and pull her inside.

"What are you doing here?" I demand.

She is frightened. I have a strong grip on her neck.

"I was coming to see if you needed anything, my lady."

"You lie. You were waiting outside my door. Why?"

She wiggles her head. "No, my lady, I am here to serve you."

"You are here to spy on me." I choke her. "Did Lord Landulf send you?"

She gasps. "No. Please? You are hurting me."

I tighten my grip and she begins to lose color. "You feel how strong I am? I have the strength of a dozen men. Tell me the truth now or you will die in pain. Were you spying outside my door?"

She can hardly get the word out. "Yes."

"You had been told I was drugged?"

"Yes."

"Who told you?"

"Lady Cia."

"You were waiting by the door for me to pass out?"

"Yes."

"What were you going to do with me then?"

Marie turns blue. But she has enough will left to struggle.

"No!" she gasps.

I dig my fingernails into her neck, drawing blood. "You answer me or I'll rip your head off!"

She moans. "I was to take you to the sacrifice."

I loosen my grip and frown. "What sacrifice? Where?"

She struggles for air. "It is below—in the hidden chambers."

I point my finger at her. "You will take me there, through a back way. I want to see this sacrifice but I do not want to be seen. Do you understand?"

She coughs weakly. "I don't want to die."

I am grim. "You keep thinking that way."

Marie leads me through a dark passageway unconnected to the hallways and rooms of the public castle. We hardly leave my bedroom when we enter a narrow tunnel opened by touching a stone with a series of special pressures. The entrance closes behind us, and

I wonder if I would have the strength to reopen it. The effect of the drug continues to plague me. Colored lights flash and trail at the corners of my vision. My heart pounds in my head and I cannot stop yawning. Cramps grip my spine. The power of the poison stuns me. Ordinarily, my system is immune to any kind of abusive substance.

We reach steep stairs and start down. The walls continue to press in on us. The stairs are seemingly endless. I carry a torch in one hand, grip the back of Marie's neck with the other. "If you cry out at any time," I say, "that cry will be the last sound you hear in this world."

"I won't betray you," she whispers.

"I can see you are very loyal."

We continue to go down for the next twenty minutes, and I begin to believe Landulf has fashioned his castle over a natural cave. It is ridiculous to think he could have carved away so much stone with human hands. Yet somebody must have built this passageway, and I have to wonder if it is older than I imagined. The surrounding stones appear ancient. I remember Dante's remark, that this spot used to shelter the Oracle of Venus.

Eventually I detect a red glow ahead. At the same time the temperature increases sharply. Putting out my torch, I stop Marie and question her.

"Lord Landulf performs sacrifices down there?" I ask.

"Yes."

"What kind?"

"All kinds."

I shake her. "Does he kill humans? Torture them?"

"Yes. Yes."

"Why?"

She weeps. "I don't know why."

"Then why do you stay here? Are you not a Christian?"

She trembles beneath my gaze. "If I do not serve, I will be sacrificed."

"Is that the law?"

"Yes. Please let me go."

"Not until I am finished with you. Is there a place from where we can watch these sacrifices? And not be detected?"

She glances in the direction of the red glow. It is as if the light of hell beckons us. I smell burnt flesh again, and it has the odor of fresh meat. Marie is having trouble breathing.

"There is a passageway off to the side and above," she whispers. "But it is not all stone."

"What do you mean?"

"It is a metal grill, set in the ceiling. If they look up, they will see us."

"Why should they look up?"

"The eyes of my lord are everywhere!"

"Shh. Don't call him your lord. He is a perverted human." I turn toward the red glow. "He will die this very night." I grab her by the neck again. "Come, you will see."

The passageway Marie speaks of comes well before we reach the cavern. I feel and hear the hot tension in the cavern, the sound of many people whispering among themselves, the moans of a few unfortunates, the faint clash of metal. Even before I see, I know Landulf has brought his devotees as well as his soldiers to this accursed hole. I have to wonder if they're not all Satan worshippers.

Marie leads me into a tunnel where we have to get down on our hands and knees and crawl. The way is hot and soon I am drenched with sweat. But below our hands and knees the stone finally turns to wire mesh. We have reached the grills from which we can peer down at what is to be.

The ceremony is about to begin.

We are directly above the altar. It is circular, surrounded on all sides by rows of pews that lead up and back one hundred feet. There are approximately six hundred people present. Each person wears a red robe, except for a few soldiers at the doors, who have on metal breast plates and helmets. The altar is black and polished; it appears to be made of marble. Inlaid is a silver pentagram. The five tips of the stars dissect the room into five sections. Landulf sits on the floor with his wife. He is the only one wearing a black robe, and I can't help but notice the small silver knife resting in his lap.

Candles surround the altar. They are black and very tall, but what is most remarkable is that they burn with purple flames. The sober light spills over the marble and the silent participants like a glow from an unearthed volcano. The tension in the air is palpable and it is not something I would wish to touch. I sense that Landulf strives for tension in his rites.

Landulf stands and walks to the center of the pentagram.

He raises his hand with the knife.

The group begins to sing, and for a moment I am bewildered. For it sounds to me as if they are singing the Catholic Mass in Latin. But then I realize they have started at the end, and are working their way toward the beginning, moving verse by verse through the litany. And the knife Landulf holds—the handle is shaped like a crucifix, yet he grasps it by the blade, upside down.

Everything they are doing is backward.

Landulf's grip is tight on his blade. Blood runs down his arm as his worshippers sing, but he doesn't seem to mind. In all of this, the most amazing thing is that their voices are quite beautiful. They remind me of Dante, who never went to sleep without reciting the Mass. Yet their motives are clearly the opposite of Dante's. He implored God for forgiveness for sins he had never committed. These creatures implore another power to accept their sins and reward them for them.

After forty minutes the twisted mass ends. A wooden cross is brought out by soldiers and laid in the center of the pentagram. Clad in a white robe, a bound female is carried out next. Her mouth is tied, she cannot cry out. But I see it is one of the girls I thought I had saved. That must mean the other two did not escape either. The girl is spread out on the cross but her white robe is left on. Finally the material stuffed in her mouth is removed and she cries out weakly. Landulf stands over her like the Grim Reaper, or worse. He has exchanged his knife for a small hammer and a bunch of nails. His intention is painfully obvious.

He is going to crucify the young woman.

I cannot watch this. I cannot let it happen.

But I have to watch. And I know I can do nothing.

Landulf holds nails and hammer up for all to see. So far the group has been fairly sedate, but now they leap to their feet and start screaming and jeering. I cannot tell if they are experiencing pain or pleasure. It seems a perverse mixture of both. Landulf kneels beside the girl and the soldiers who hold her down as the noise of the group reaches a frenzy. The very air is now vibrating. I find myself panting hard, on the verge of vomiting. I am a vampire who has killed thousands, yet I cannot bear that they should do this *thing* to such innocence, and enjoy it, and still remain human. It doesn't seem as if God should allow it.

I have to remind myself that God allowed it long ago.

Landulf begins to hammer in the nails.

The blood flows over the silver pentagram.

The girl's screams rend my soul.

Then I cry out, and the group falls instantly silent.

Plump, frightened Marie has stabbed a knife in my lower back. Put it in deep, cut a few arteries and important nerves. My blood seeps over the wire mesh and spills onto the altar below. Directly on to Landulf's face. He stares up and hungrily licks it as it drops—rain from hell. There is poison on the tip of Marie's blade; it mingles with the drugs already racking my system and causes havoc with my reflexes. Straining to pull it out, I feel my wound being licked by this docile servant girl. She has been told something about my blood, and thinks it will grant her immortality and great powers. She is like a giant insect sticking a needle in my vital organs. But apparently she takes the feeding ritual too far. Landulf suddenly shouts at her.

"It is for me!" he yells.

I am in such agony. Without wishing it, my weight and Marie's weight sag onto the wire mesh. It breaks. We fall like creatures cast down from heaven. Marie lands on her head and her skull explodes in a gray mass. I land on my back and the knife rams so deeply into me that it pokes through my liver and out my front. I have crashed beside the half-crucified woman, and Landulf steps over her to get to me. His face is smeared with blood, yet incredibly he appears sad, as if he wished it could have ended another way. I feel I have reached the end. My strength ebbs rapidly; I cannot get the knife out of my back, so that I may heal. The tortured girl screams at me as if I were a demon. Her mind is shattered. On the cold black altar our blood mingles and flows over the silver star as the crowd cheers. All this had been entertainment to them. Landulf puts a foot on my bloody hair and stares down at me.

"How do you feel, Sita?" he asks with feeling.

I cough blood. "Wonderful."

"You have come to where I always wanted you to be."

I try to roll on to my side, still trying for the blade.

He steps on my free arm with his other foot.

"I am happy for you," I gasp.

He grins slowly. "You are very beautiful, your body, your spirit. This agony is unnecessary. Join me, I will remove the knife and you will be better."

The pain is unbearable. "What do I have to do to join you?"

He presses hard on my arm, grinding the bone into the floor.

"A small thing," he replies. "Just finish nailing these stakes in this young woman you foolishly tried to save."

I think about it for a moment.

A long moment considering my situation.

"My lord," I say. "Go to hell."

He laughs and raises his foot and puts it over my face.

Darkness comes. It is especially dark.

13 ~~~

When I come to, I feel as if I am being crucified. There is pain in my arms and chest, and I can hardly breathe. Opening my eyes, I find myself chained in a cell, deep in a black dungeon. My arms are strung above me, spread out like the wings of a bird, pinned to a dripping stone wall with locks similar to the ones I saw on the cage. This metal is a special alloy that I am unable to break, at least in my present condition. I struggle with the binds and only end up exhausting myself further.

Naturally, I can still see in the dark. From head to foot, I am covered with blood, but I see that it is not my blood, but that of the girl they were sacrificing. The knife has been removed from my spine and that wound has healed. But there is no relief for me.

Crucifixion brings death by slow suffocation, and the position of my arms and legs mimics that of the Roman style of execution. My feet are also bound to the wall, but they are slightly above the floor so that all the pressure of the metal anklets is on my calf bones. Remnants of Landulf's poisons continue to percolate in my system. I have to wonder if he siphoned off large amounts of my blood while I was unconscious.

Yet I do not think so.

How long I have been hanging there, I do not know. But steadily my pain grows so great that I begin to cry quietly to myself. Yes, even I, ancient Sita, who has faced the trials of four thousand years of life and survived, feel as if I have at last been defeated. Each breath is an exercise in cruel labor; the air burns my chest as it is forced in, and each time I exhale, I wonder if I will have the strength to squeeze in another lungful. My cries turn to feeble screams, then moans that reverberate deep in my soul, like the solemn laminations of the dammed already sealed in hell. I feel I have been forced beneath the earth, into a place of unceasing punishment. Landulf's face swims in my mind and I wonder if I see a vision of Satan.

Yet in my suffering, on the verge of final unconsciousness, something remarkable happens. My mind begins to clear, and I remember Alanda and Suzama, Seymour and the child. I see the stars and recall how I floated high above the Earth, and swore to do everything I could to protect my mother world. I am five thousand years old, not four thousand. I am from the future and I have returned in time to defeat Landulf. And I will defeat him, I tell myself. He will come for me, I remember he did before. I just have to hang on a little while longer.

I remember other things as well.

The Spear of Longinus.

I remember it from twentieth century Europe.

In Austria, in the year 1927, in the capital city of Vienna, I saw Richard Wagner's opera *Parsival,* which portrayed the adventures of King Arthur's knights in search of the Holy Grail, in a mythological setting. Historians claimed at that time that there was no historical basis for the events in the opera. Still, Richard Wagner's masterpiece was very moving, the powerful music, the tragic plot of how the knights struggled against the evil Klingsor, who obstructed them at every step from behind the scenes. Most of all, I was intrigued by Wagner's use of the Spear of Longinus—which I had seen in *my* past—as a magic wand in the hands of the evil Klingsor.

It made me realize, *then,* that Klingsor might have been Landulf.

There could be historical accuracy in the opera, after all.

After leaving the theater, I researched Wagner's source material and read Wolfram von Eschenbach's *Parsival,* upon which the opera was based. I was intrigued to see that the spear played an even more central role in the actual tale, and was stunned to learn that Eschenbach had lived eleven generations after the time of Arthur and Parsival, and yet had managed to write a thrilling story even though he was supposedly an illiterate imbecile. From what could be gleaned from the old texts, it seemed that Eschenbach had simply cognized—out of the thin air—the mystical tale.

Even then, in the twentieth century in Austria, that fact had made me wonder if perhaps Eschenbach's story was symbolic of deeper truths. Because by the twentieth century, history had all but forgotten Landulf. Yet even Eschenbach, a wandering Homer of little reputation, a *minnesinger,* had named him the most evil man who had ever lived. Who knew better than I why Eschenbach should condemn the duke so? Chilled by my own memories, I became convinced that Klingsor was indeed Landulf.

In the story, Klingsor had been an archbishop who lived at Kalot Enbolot, in southwest Sicily, where he summoned demons and sent them forth to torment the world. But most important, Eschenbach had described Klingsor's most important identifying mark and the basis of his evil.

Yet, in Landulf's dark prison, I cannot remember that mark.

From far away, as I become more delirious, I hear a sound. Knights and lords approaching from above, slowly winding down to my black cell. My torment is unbearable—for it to end, it seems, is all I can hope for. Yet I force in a shuddering breath and steel myself to fulfill my promise to those who sent me back in time. I recall Krishna's promise to me, that his grace shall always be with me. But I do not ask God to save me, only to give me the strength to save myself.

The door opens and in strides Landulf.

Alone. His men wait outside.

He brings a clean damp towel and wipes at the blood that has dried on my face. Then he touches my cheek, and before I can react, leans forward and plants a kiss on my cracked lips. I try to spit in his face, but there is not enough moisture in my mouth.

Landulf stares at me with such compassion that I have to wonder if I have slipped into a dream where demons are angels and the future is already burned to ash by our ancestors' sins. For moment I am in more than one time, but then Landulf slaps me hard on the cheek, even as he pretends to bemoan my torment, and then I am alone with him, only him.

"Sita," he says with sympathy. "Why do you do this to yourself?"

I strain to moisten my swollen throat. "I could swear, my lord, that I did not climb into these chains while I was unconscious."

He enjoys my gusto. "But these chains are of your own making. I have offered you another way. Why don't you take it? What is the sacrifice for one such as you? We are already old partners in this war."

"I didn't know that this was a war?" I say honestly.

He is serious. "But it is—a battle far older than even your nonperishable body. It goes back to the birth of the stars, to the dropping of the veil, and of the opening of the two paths back to the source. You see me as a monster but I tell you I am God's greatest devotee."

"Aren't you exaggerating just a little?"

He slaps me again. "No! It is the truth you refuse to see. Will is stronger than love. Power lasts longer than virtue. My path is left-handed, true, but it is the swiftest and the surest." He pauses and comes closer. "Did not your friends tell you that all roads lead to the same destination?"

His question stuns me, the implications of his insight. "What friends are those?" I ask innocently.

He nods to himself as he studies my eyes. "I have seen you before on the path."

I force a smile and know it must more closely resemble a grimace. "Then you must know I will never join you. Because althought I may be a sinner, I am also a servant. I love virtue, I love human love, even if I am not human. These are the things that bring me the most joy. Your path may be swift and sure but it is barren. The desert surrounds your every step and you walk forever a thirsty man. You may leave me to rot in this cell, but I am not forsaken. When I leave this body I know I will drink deep of Christ's and Krishna's fathomless love, and I will be happy while you crawl on your hands and knees to invoke your miserable demons. Whom you send out to perform deeds you are too frightened to perform in person. You sicken me, Landulf. Had I a free hand, I would tear your tongue from your face so that you could no longer spew lies in my direction."

He is unmoved by my speech.

"You will beg for my mercy, Sita. You will kill at my bidding."

I snort. "You will not live long enough, my lord, to see me do either."

He holds my eye. "We shall see." He raises a hand and snaps a finger and two armor-clad soldiers with torches, a prisoner between them, waddle into the cell.

They have brought Dante.

"My lady!" he cries when he sees me and tries to run to my side. But he trips and falls facedown on the damp floor, and is only able to rise when Landulf pulls him up by his hair. The black lord shoves my friend in my direction and Dante cowers and prays at my feet, weeping to see me in such a desperate condition. I would weep for my friend if there were any tears left in my body. But all I can do is sigh and shake my head.

"Dante," I say. "I told you to go back to Messina. Why are you here?"

He clasps my foot. "I could not leave you, my lady. I will never leave you."

Landulf is grim. "We caught him outside the castle walls, groveling like an animal." He grabs him by the neck and picks him all the way up off the floor with one hand. The demonstration of strength disturbs me. Perhaps he did take my blood, and put it into his veins, while I was unconscious. Yet Landulf does not show the signs of being a true vampire. He dangles Dante in front of me. "Will you not beg, Sita?" Landulf asks me.

I am fearful. "For what?"

"You know, my proud ruby."

I sneer. "Why beg for that which does not exist?"

In response Landulf throws Dante down in a heap and takes a torch from one of his men. Knocking out the flame on the damp wall, he steps toward Dante with the embers of the torch top still glowing. Seeing what Landulf has in mind, Dante tries to scamper to me but is kicked aside by Landulf. The evil lord kneels by my friend and points out to me Dante's sores.

"These wounds are infected," Landulf says. "They must be cauterized and sealed. Don't you agree, Sita?"

I stare in horror. "He served you loyally for many years."

Landulf eyes Dante, who trembles in anticipation.

"But he betrayed me in the end," he says. "And it is only the end that matters, not the manner of the path."

"Landulf!" I cry.

But he ignores me, and then Dante is crying, screaming for me to save him as if I were his mother. But even though I have returned in time with the wisdom of the ages, I can do nothing—cannot keep Landulf from pressing the embers into Dante's oozing sores. Landulf first does my friend's deformed hand, and then he moves toward Dante's leg, where the damage is even more extensive. Dante howls so loud and hard it seems as if his skull will explode. Certainly the sound threatens to rupture my own heart. As Landulf moves forward with the torch again, I hear myself cry out.

"Please?" I yell. "Please stop!"

Landulf pauses and smiles up at me. "You beg me?"

I nod weakly. "I beg you, my lord."

Landulf stands. "Good. You have passed the first step of initiation. The second step will come later, and then the final and third step." He gestures to Dante, on the floor, who appears to have gone into shock. He speaks to his knights. "Chain this bag of garbage up beside her. Let them keep each other company, and let them talk together about the redeeming and saving power of love and mercy." Landulf winks at me as he leaves the dungeon. "I will see you soon, Sita."

14 ～～

More time goes by and with each passing minute I die a little more inside. Crucified alone in the dark, I could imagine no crueler torture, yet I had not known the half of it. Dante is largely unconscious, but still he moans miserably. For a time I pray that he does not wake again, that he simply dies, and so ends his suffering. But then the curse of all who suffer comes to me.

I glimpse a faint ray of hope.

I have to wake Dante, bring him back to the nightmare.

Calling his name softly, he finally stirs and raises his head and looks around. It is so dark; it is obvious he cannot see a thing. But I can see his ruined expression and it pierces my heart. He is hung up on the wall right beside me.

"Sita?" he whispers.

"I am here," I say gently. "Don't be afraid."

He is having trouble breathing. Landulf's knights have tied him up like me, his arms pinned by unbreakable chains. Yet his feet are not bound; they manage to touch the floor. But I know soon he will begin to smother. He coughs as he tries to speak.

"I'm sorry, my lady," he says. "I disobeyed you."

"No. You have nothing to be ashamed of. You are a true hero. Even when the situation appears hopeless, you plunge forward. Perseus himself, I would guess, would be envious of your stout heart."

He tries to smile. "Could it be true?"

"Oh yes. And you might yet save us both."

He is interested. "How, my lady?"

"I need you to shake free of your leg brace and push it over here."

"My lady?"

"Your tiny copper crucifix, the one you pray to before sleeping each night. I need it."

He is worried. "What are you going to do to it?"

"I am sorry, Dante, I am going to have to ruin it. But I think I can form the cross into a narrow instrument that I can use to pick these locks."

"But, my lady, your hands are bound!"

"I am going to use my toes to mold it into a proper shape. Don't worry about the details, Dante, just push your brace over here. Is it easy to slip out of?"

"No problem, my lady." I see him struggle in the dark. "Are you on my right or on my left?"

I have to smile. "I am on your left, two feet away."

"I feel you near," he says with affection as he slips

out of the brace and pushes it toward me with his stump. "Do you have it?"

"No. My feet are pinned together. You will have to give it a shove, but not too hard. The brace must come to rest against the side of my legs."

"But I can't see your legs."

"They are pinned to the wall. Lay the brace against the wall and just give it a slight nudge forward."

"Are you sure this is a good plan?"

"Yes."

"I am not sure."

"Dante?"

He suddenly hyperventilates. "I am afraid, my lady! Without my brace I will be a cripple!"

I speak soothingly. "I will not damage your brace, Dante. Only the cross you keep hidden in it. When I am free, you will have your brace back and we will escape from here."

He begins to calm. "We will go back to Messina?"

"Yes. Together we will travel to Messina, and there we will stay in the finest inn, and order the best food and wine. You will be my companion and I will tell everyone how you rescued me from the evil duke."

Dante beams. "I will be like Perseus! I will slay the Gorgon!"

"Exactly. But let's get out of here first. Push the brace closer to me."

"What if I push it too far?"

"You won't, Dante. You are a hero. Heroes don't make mistakes."

Dante pushes feebly at the brace with his leper stump. "Is that all right, my lady?"

"Harder."

"I am trying, my lady." He strikes the brace with

his stump and the wooden leg bumps up against my calf. "You have it?"

"I have it," I quickly reassure him. "You relax and catch your breath. You don't even have to speak to me. I will concentrate on getting us out of here."

He groans. "Hurry, my lady. I am in some pain."

"I know, my friend."

Even for a vampire, what I plan to do next is not easy. First I have to let the top of the brace slide down to where I can reach it with my toes. This I do without much effort, but Dante's cross is not stored at the top of the brace. It is fastened somewhat deeper inside the wooden stump. After fishing for it with my toes for ten minutes, I am no closer to reaching it, and even more weary, if that is possible.

Then it occurs to me that I must invert the brace. This is tricky, because if the copper cross slips past my toes, it will land on the floor and be out of reach. What I do to add a safety margin to my plan is to raise the brace up with just one foot, catching it between my big toe and the toe next to it. Then I plug the end of the brace with the bottom of my other foot. Shaking the brace upside down in the air, at a ninety-degree angle to my calf, I feel the cross touch the sole of my free foot. In a moment my toes have a grip on the crucifix and I let go of the brace.

"My lady?" Dante cries.

"Everything is all right."

"My brace is not broken?"

"It is fine. Be silent and conserve your strength. We will soon be free."

"Yes, my lady."

Both my feet grip the copper cross. I will keep plenty of toes wrapped around it at all times, I tell myself. There is no way it is going to spring beyond my reach. As I work to mold the copper, I pray Landulf's *soon* did not mean in the next few minutes. I have prayed many times since entering the castle.

The crucifix is relatively thin, little more than a stamped plate, and this is fortunate. It does not take me long to squeeze the lower portion of the cross into a stiff wire. True, it is a rather plump wire but the key holes in the locks that bind me are far from tiny. Clasping the wire in my right foot, and holding still the key hole with my left foot, I slowly glide the cooper toward the inner mechanism.

"My lady?"

"Shh, Dante. Patience."

"My hand pains me."

"We will make it better soon. Please do not speak for the next few minutes."

The wire enters the lock and I feel around to get a sense of its design. My mind is very alert now. The traumas I have suffered—I put them all behind so I can focus on the inside of the lock. It does not take long before I have a complete mental picture of how it was built, and when I do, I know precisely how to move my wire.

There is a click and the lock springs open.

I kick off the chains. My feet are free.

"My lady!" Dante cheers.

"Quiet. Let me finish."

He gasps. "Oh, yes, hurry. I cannot breathe like this."

Now comes the hardest part. I cannot pull either hand chain down close enough to my face so that I might work the locks with the wire between my teeth, assuming I could get the copper in my mouth. No, I have to reach up with my right foot, stretching my leg to a next-to-impossible length, and attack the *left* lock that way. My muscles are stiff so the task is doubly hard. Yet I can taste freedom now, and it gives me fresh strength.

Clenching the wire in my toes, I kick up.

My hamstring muscles scream.

I fail to reach the lock. I have to kick up a dozen times before I even approach it. But steadily my joints limber, and finally I am steering the wire into the lock that grips my left wrist. Since I already know the internal design of the mechanism, I take only a second to trip it. My left hand is now free, and I immediately transfer the wire from my toes into my fingers. Two seconds after that, I have sprung the right lock and am able to stand and stretch. But Dante has gone downhill. He doesn't even realize that I am free. I step to his side and caress the top of his head. He looks up without seeing me in the pitch black and smiles.

"Are we safe?" he asks softly.

"Almost," I say, and I use the wire to open his locks. But his arms don't come down when they are free, his limbs are so damaged. I have to draw them down, and this makes him cry out. He buries his face in my chest and I comfort him. "Dante," I say. "This dungeon will not hold us."

He lets go of me, but he is lost in the dark and he cannot stand without support. "Where is my brace?" he asks. "Will it still work?"

"Your brace is here and it is undamaged, as I promised." I slide his stump back into it but cringe at the smell of his burnt flesh. Taking his wounded left hand, I study the sores. Landulf took his cauterization too far; he burned into the healthy tissue beneath

Dante's wounds. Later, I swear to myself, when we have time, I must sprinkle a few drops of my blood on the sores to ease his agony.

"It is best you don't touch me, my lady" Dante says in shame.

I squeeze his arm. "You are my hero. Of course I will touch you."

He is happy, for the moment, but he is also close to death.

"My lady," he gasps as he continues to struggle for air, despite his release from the bonds. "I know a secret the duke might not even know." He taps the wall behind his head. "There is a passageway back here, if we can get to it. The way leads under the farthest wall and out into the woods."

"Can we reach this passageway from the tunnel beyond this cell door?"

"Yes, my lady. But how are we going to get through the door?"

Good question. After studying the door, I see that it is made of the same alloy as the locks and chains. I cannot break through it. But I have come to this dilemma before. My awareness of the future is still present, but still somewhat cloudy. For several seconds I cannot remember precisely what I did next. Then the water dripping from the wall against which we were imprisoned catches my attention. The mortar between the stones must be weak, I reason, to allow so much moisture to seep through it and into the cell.

"Dante," I say. "Is this secret passageway of yours flooded?"

"Sometimes, my lady. At certain times of the year."

"Is this a certain time of the year?"

He hesitates. "There should be some water in the

passage, yes. But I do not think it will be flooded. I hope it is not."

"Does the water run out into the forest?"

"The passageway leads in two directions. The water runs out to the cliff, in the direction of the sea."

"Stand away from this wall, by the door. I am going to work on these stones."

"Yes, my lady. Where is the door?"

I have to lead him to it. He slides down, weakly, with his back to the exit. He cannot stop moving his left hand, and I can only imagine the pain it must be causing him.

Landulf has removed my shoes, but this does not stop me from leaping in the air and kicking at one of the stones with my right heel. It cracks with a single hard blow, and a series of kicks crush it. I pull out the chunks of stone and mortar with my hands, and soon I have a small river running through my fingers and over my lap. Yet I see the passageway is slightly above us, and that there is not more than a foot of water passing through it. Dante shivers and cries out as the cold water touches him and I have to talk to reassure him. My hands are frantically busy, pulling out pieces of stone. My strength level has gone up another notch. We were both so close to death, everything was hopeless, and now we stand on freedom's door.

Soon there is a hole large enough for us to crawl through. I help Dante into the passageway, and then I follow him. Soon I am standing beside him, steadying him with my hand. The water current is feeble; even Dante is able to stand against it. He grabs my arm and points upstream.

"This way is the woods, my lady," he says. "Soon we will be free of this unholy place."

I stop him. "I can't go with you, Dante, not yet."

His exhilaration turns to distress. "My lady? Why not?"

"I cannot go from here and leave Landulf alive."

Dante is devastated. "But if you go after him you will die! He is too strong!"

"I am strong, Dante. You have seen that. But I need your help to find him. Where does he spend most of his time in the castle?"

Dante is animated. "No, my lady. I don't know. He is like most people and moves around from place to place. You will not find him before his knights find you. Please, we must escape now while we have a chance."

I clasp his shoulders. "But I have to try to find him, Dante. Landulf may have taken something from me, something very precious, and I cannot leave this castle without knowing that he has been destroyed."

Dante is confused. "What did he take from you that is so precious?"

"I cannot explain that to you. I just need you to trust me that I speak the truth. Come, you spent many years with him. Where is the most likely place he will be right now?"

"But I don't know when right now is, my lady. All is dark in here."

I stop and concentrate. Even though I have been unconscious much of the time, my very cells remember the passage of time. "It is the second morning after I came here, not long before dawn." I pause. "Where does he spend his mornings?"

Dante's face twitches. "If I tell you, will you do what you did last time? Will you go to him?"

I stroke his head and speak in a gentle hypnotic

voice. "You have to tell me. You are my friend. You are the only one I can trust. It is imperative that I destroy Landulf before I leave here. Not merely for the safety of you and me, but for the well-being of all people everywhere. You can see that, can't you? His evil has spread far and wide. I must stop it here at its source."

My words go deep into Dante. "He causes much suffering in many lands," he whispers as he nods to himself.

"And that suffering can stop today. Tell me where in this castle he spends his mornings?"

"But, my lady, if you leave me now, when will I see you again?"

I continue to stroke his head. "Remember the pool of water where we slept the night before we came to the castle? It was off the road. Do you think you would be able to hike back there?"

He nods vigorously. "I can do it. I know these woods. When will you meet me there?"

"This evening. I can get there by then. Can you?"

"I am sure of it, my lady. If I do not stop to rest."

"You can stop to rest. If I get there before you, I will wait."

He grips my arm fiercely. "Do you promise, my lady?"

"I promise you, Dante. With all my heart." I pause and sharpen my tone. I know my next words must feel as if they cut right through him like knives but the time has passed for gentle persuasion. "Now tell me where Landulf is."

Dante speaks quickly, startled. "He is probably not in the castle now. He spends most mornings at the ancient oracle, where Venus was long ago venerated."

"Where is this spot?" I demand.

"It is a stone circle built into the side of the cliff at the back of the castle." He gestures downstream. "That way opens onto a stream that falls not far from the place. But it is a dangerous spot, my lady. His power is greatest there, and the spirits protect him. You will not be able to get to him. You have to wait until he leaves the circle."

"We will see." I pat Dante on the back. "Before this day is through, you and I will meet again. It will be a time of rejoicing. The evil enemy will be defeated and good friends will be together and free to go where they wish."

"To Messina?" he asks excitedly.

"Yes, we can go to Messina." I hug him. "Take care of yourself, Dante. You are much loved by me."

He hugs me in return and speaks in my ear.

"You are my love, my lady."

15 〜〜

The dark path leads to light, but the sun is not yet up when I exit the underground passageway and stand on the edge of the cliff and look out at the vast panorama. A large section of the south shore of Sicily is indeed visible. The sea is purple and there are few clouds. The closest beach—far below and perhaps three miles distant—is occupied by a large contingent of soldiers. I can see the color of their skin, their black and green flags that wave in the morning breeze.

Arabs. Moslems.

They could not be so near without Lord Landulf's consent.

The duke is not far away, off to my left, down about five hundred feet. As Dante warned, he sits in the center of a circle of stones—defined by the shape of the ledge and the pointed rocks that enclose it—in another pentagram. This five-pointed star appears to have been drawn by blood, and there is something red and slimy in his hands. He sits on his knees with his back to the cliff and I do not know what thoughts run through his corrupt mind. I only know he will be dead in a few minutes.

I start down the cliff.

Venus shines bright in the eastern sky.

I take her white light as a good omen.

I come within fifty feet of the stone circle before I pause. There is a young woman chained to the cliff just below me, and I see Landulf has the Spear of Longinus with him at the center of the pentagram. I find it odd that I did not see it at first since I have not let him out of my sight on the hike down the cliff. But the fact does not concern me; the girl does. She is the one who assisted me when I rescued her and her friends from the cage. Like her friend, who was sacrificed at the black mass, she wears a white robe and looks terrified. Yet except for the three of us, I sense no one else in the vicinity. I descend another thirty feet, silently, staring at Landulf's back. I know it is him. The girl sees me and I motion for her to remain silent. Her eyes are suddenly wide with hope, and I have to wonder if that is good. This all seems too easy.

Then I pause again. Something makes me sick.

Lady Cia lies not far from the chained girl.

Her heart has been cut from her chest.

Now I know what Lord Landulf holds in his hands.

He continues to sit with his back to me. Defenseless.

"It was necessary, Sita," he says softly.

That he knows I am here stuns me.

"Why?" I ask.

He glances over his shoulder.

"The sacrifice demanded the ultimate sacrifice," he says.

"To achieve what aim?" I ask.

"To bring you here, to this spot."

I snort. "I brought myself here, thank you. None of your demons assisted me."

He stands and stares at me. His wife's heart continues to drip in his open palm. His eyes are so dark "That's what you think," he says quietly.

I gesture to the girl. "Why is she here?"

"For you. For the next step in your initiation."

I point to my ears. "I have sensitive hearing. The three of us are alone on this cliff. Not that it matters. You would need an army to protect you from what I am going to do to you now."

He gestures to the circle, using the heart. "You say your ears are sensitive. What about your eyes? Can you not see what you are up against?"

Now that he mentions it, I do notice a peculiar vibration in the air. It's as if we're surrounded by a swarm of insects, yet there is no sound. The sensation of the swarm is psychological. Now I feel as if something foul picks at my skin. I start to brush it away, but stop myself. I fear to show weakness in front of him. Yet a faint thread of fear has already entered my mind, and slowly begun to wrap around the center of my brain. However, I still feel I have the upper hand. I am an ancient vampire of incredible strength. He is just a man. Why, he doesn't even have his spear in his hand to protect himself.

I step toward the stone circle and bump into a barrier.

It is invisible but palpable. A wall.

Or a magnetic force that resists physical contact.

I pound on it with my fist to no effect.

Landulf grins at me from inside the circle.

"To enter," he says. "You will have to sacrifice an innocent."

The girl cries behind me. I silence her with a gesture.

"That will never happen," I say as I slowly probe the perimeter of the stone circle, seeking for a weak spot. But the force field is uniform, and I am amazed that it even exists. My memories of the future are back again, clearer than ever. I have to wonder if the shield is of extraterrestrial origin. The last time I confronted Landulf on this spot, I defeated him by using his wife as a shield. This is the first event that is being played out differently from the last time. So I know I must have come back in time for this final moment.

Yet I do not know what to do.

Landulf follows my movements and does nothing to thwart me. I complete my inspection of the circle and pause to consider the possibility of jumping into the circle from the side of the cliff. Landulf reads my mind, or perhaps he logically figures out what my next move must be.

"You can try it," he says. "I would enjoy watching you bounce off the edge of the cliff."

"You cannot stay in there forever," I reply.

"Dante cannot stay in the underground passageway forever."

I freeze. "You bluff. You cannot stop him from here."

In response Landulf raises the heart toward the sky and to my amazement it starts beating. The blood squirts on his face and he licks it. Then he lets out a high-pitched cackle, and I hear a loud shifting of stone far above. Glancing up the way I came, I see that the exit to the cliff has been closed over with a fallen boulder. Landulf lowers the heart.

"That is one end," he warns. "I can close the other end the same way. If . . ."

He doesn't finish. He wants me to.

"If I don't come get you," I say.

"Exactly." He gestures to the chained girl, who is not enjoying the display of the duke's powers. "The life of your friend for the life of a stranger."

I glance at the girl and she shakes her head slightly.

"Don't worry," I snap at her.

"You need to rip out her heart," Landulf explains. "Quickly. While it still beats, you will be able to penetrate the circle."

"I do not barter in human lives." But sudden doubt plagues me. If I do not kill him, he will kill the girl anyway. And I will not be able to take her with me down the side of the sheer cliff. Dante's innocent face haunts me, as do Landulf's hypnotic eyes. I just want to get to the duke and scratch his face off to put an end to his circus. He moves to the edge of the circle, comes within five feet of where I stand. Once more I pound on the barrier but my fists rebound against my chest. His dead wife's heart continues to beat and now the sound is in my ears. I do not understand how his palm can animate it. How a wizard, no matter how powerful, can infuse life into what should be dead.

"You will barter," he promises. "Fool! There is no part of you I cannot touch. No aspect of you I cannot defile." He stops. "Hear something, Sita?"

The beating of the heart grows louder in my ears.

In my head. Even when I cover my ears it doesn't help.

He shoves the heart toward me and I am forced to stare at it.

This is madness—I cannot even close my eyes.

"Kill her and it will stop," he says.

"No!" I cry.

"Kill her and your friend will live! Kill her and you can kill me!"

The blood of the pounding heart splashes through the barrier and catches my face. I taste the waste of Cia's perverted life on my lips and the pounding in my head increases ten-fold. Surely I will go mad if I do not stop it in the next few seconds. Whirling toward the chained girl, I do not know what she hears except that she suddenly screams. Maybe the sight of my crazed expression makes her scream. What is one human life, I think? In four thousand years I have murdered thousands, ripped the lives from a parade of innocents. I need her heart, just for a second. Her sacrifice is necessary to spare the torment of billions in the future. She should be happy to die for such a noble cause. God should see that I have no choice in the matter.

But he will not see that and I know it.

Because I am five—not four—thousand years old.

I know to murder innocents is to murder my own soul.

But the pounding grows louder.

It is a miracle Landulf's voice can be heard above it.

"You can rip out my heart when you are done with me," he says. "And then you will finally be at peace. Peace, Sita!"

My body balls up in pain.

I squeeze my ears between my knees.

The beat of the dead heart. Nothing can stop it.

Tears run over my face. Bloody tears.

The girl swims in my red vision.

My head will explode, I know.

"Kill her, Sita!" Landulf implores.

My mission will fail. Billions will burn.

"Rip out her heart!"

In my head. The pain. The pounding. Please.

"Do it!"

I do it. Finally, just this once, I listen to him.

Leaping toward her, giving her almost no time to react, I thrust my left hand into her chest, smashing through her white gown and her pale ribs. Yet for a fraction of a second, she knows what I am going to do. She feels the absolute horror of the ritual execution. That is what Landulf wants, what he needs, to activate his black sorcery. The battery of the bastard is tied to perversity and pain. The girl's heart is in my hand. I feel its life, and still I yank it from her chest and leap toward the circle. Out the corner of my eye I see her staring at me, and understand the betrayal she is feeling deep in my soul. Her eyes are as blue as mine. Even in death, they could be mine.

I land inside the circle, at the tip of a point on the pentagram.

The pounding stops. The agony in my head.

The dead girl's heart seems to melt in my hand.

Landulf has picked up the mystical spear.

"They are always hungry," he explains as he nods toward the heart vaporizing in my left palm. In moments it is entirely gone. There is not even a stain of blood left on my hand. Landulf raises the spear and takes a step toward me. He is pleased with me. "You have passed the second step," he says.

I ready myself for his attack. I shift to the right side. My foot touches fire.

I whip my foot back. There are no visible flames.

"You are now in hell," Landulf says. "You are required to stay inside the lines of the pentagram. But I am free to roam where I wish, all over the circle."

He lunges at me with the spear. He is fast.

I leap over to the adjacent star point.

He barely misses me. He flashes me a smile.

"Isn't this fun?" he asks.

"Delightful," I say.

"There is one other rule you should know. Don't jump or walk through the center of the pentagram. There is an invisible being waiting there that might consume you alive."

"You expect me to believe you?" I ask.

"You don't have to. But then, I will lose you forever, and you will be trapped in a dark place forever." He raises the spear once more. "But do what you want. You may even try to escape from the circle, but you won't be able to. Once you are in here with me, you will stay in here."

He makes another stab at me. I leap to the next point on the star. He misses, but I realize that I cannot keep on like this forever. His freedom of movement gives him a devastating advantage. His speed and strength are a mystery to me. But perhaps they come from the sum total of all the demons he carries in his heart. He is not necessarily as strong as I am, but his strength is close. I can tell by the power in his physical bursts. And he has the mystical spear, and I have to wonder if Christ's dried blood is an advantage or disadvantage in this cursed place.

"The spear is neither negative or positive," he says, maybe reading my mind, maybe guessing. "The tip is simply a point around which destiny turns. In the hands of a saint, it could be used for great healing. In my hands, it is merely a tool for my immortality."

"You are not immortal," I snap.

"But I will be, Sita. In a few moments. As soon as I pierce your side with this spear and channel your blood into my body."

"You could have done that when I was unconscious."

"No. To get the full benefit of your blood it is necessary that I drain you in my place of power. And you had to enter here of your own free will, after executing an innocent. Everything that has happened to you has been planned to bring you to this precise point." He pauses. "You see, Sita, I know you are from the future."

He continues to shock me.

"How do you know?" I gasp.

"Because I am from the same future."

"Did I know you?"

"Yes."

"Who?"

"Linda's boyfriend. I was the one who sent you into the desert."

"That fat slob?"

He is not offended. "I was in disguise."

I nod in admiration. "You are clever. More clever than any foe I have ever encountered."

My remark pleases him. He lowers the spear.

"Thank you. You have also been a worthy adversary. Why don't you let this end with dignity? I will give you that if you stop resisting me."

I sigh. "What do you want me to do?"

"Stand still for a moment. I do not need a lot of time."

"What will you do to me?" I ask.

"I will take your blood. I need your blood. But you will not have to suffer. You have my promise on that."

I consider. "All right. I will surrender on two conditions."

"What are they?"

"I want to open my own veins. And I want to use the nail that was on the cross, the one now tied to the tip of your spear."

"Why the nail?" he asks.

"Because you say it was pounded into the hand or foot of Jesus. If I am to die, I want that nail to pierce my own flesh." I add, "It will make me feel closer to him as I die."

Landulf is thoughtful. "That will not save you from what is to follow. You are already in my circle. No works of Christ function here. I am not lying to you."

"Perhaps. But those are my conditions." I shrug. "I don't ask much."

He is wary. "You could try to use the nail as a weapon. You could throw it at me."

"Would you be able to block such a throw?"

"Yes."

"Then what do you have to fear by tossing me the nail?"

"Nothing. I fear nothing in my place."

"Then toss me the nail, O Fearless One."

"You mock me?" he demands.

"Well, in the future it might be called flirting."

He hesitates. "I don't have to do this. I will get you eventually."

"Probably. But you never know."

"You believe the talisman will protect you? Despite what I say?"

"No. You are wrong there."

"Then you lie to me. You will not keep your side of the bargain."

I laugh. "You call me a fool? You have nothing to lose by trusting me." This time I catch his eye, and put all my will behind the gaze. "You will never be successful as an immortal if you live in such fear, Lord Landulf."

I have pushed the right button.

Perhaps his only button.

He hates to be called a coward.

He begin to undo the wire holding the nail in place.

"When you have the nail, you open your veins immediately," he says. "I will tolerate no delay."

"I will not waste your time," I promise.

The nail is free. He tosses it to me.

"Christian paraphernalia," he says bitterly.

I place the nail in my right palm, the tip pointed toward Landulf, and stare at it. Neither Yaksha's nor the child's nor my daughter's blood is in this present form of mine. I am strong but still only a shadow of what I will be in the future. Since returning to Sicily I have felt no power of psychokinesis, the ability to move objects with my mind. It was Kalika's blood alone that gave me that ability, and my daughter hasn't even been born yet. Still, my daughter gave her life to save the child, paid for his life with her own. And the child's blood, in an earlier reincarnation, was once on this nail. There is a connection that can reasonably be made here, or else mystically contrived. No doubt a particle of Christ's blood still remains on the metal, deep in the folds of the atoms that bind it together.

It is on this invisible blood I focus. I still believe in the miracle of this blood. My belief is born of experience. I have seen it bring a friend back to life. My belief is stronger than evil incantations spoken to cruel spirits, and bloody pentagrams drawn on forsaken cliffs. I made a serious mistake by stealing the girl's heart, but now I will give my own heart in exchange for hers. And in exchange for my life, for just a second of time, I ask for the power that my daughter already gave to me. I ask it out of favor to Kalika, whom I am sure would not want her mother to go down without a final chance of victory. Yes, I have the nerve to remind God that he owes me for my daughter's sacrifice. But I also have the faith to believe he hears me.

And my faith is stronger than stone.

Landulf lifts the spear. "You had better hurry."

I feel my mind touch the nail.

"Yes," I whisper. "Hurry."

I feel my heart touch it. Caress it.

And I know beyond all doubt it once touched Christ.

Landulf shoulders the spear. "You die now, Sita."

The nail trembles. My hand remains firm. My gaze. Power sweeps over me from way beyond the circle.

"No," I say. "Evil one, you die."

Landulf starts to let the spear fly.

The nail flies out of my palm and is impaled in his forehead.

Between his eyebrows. He stares at me through a red river.

"You," he says, and drops the spear.

I leap to his side and catch the spear before it lands.

The nail has plunged all the way in.

"I take back what I said a moment ago," I say. "You are not so clever."

I stick the spear in his heart, and his blood spurts out, even into the center of the pentagram, where it is mysteriously consumed in midair. He tries to speak one last time, probably to curse my soul for all of time, but he is staggering blindly with a long spear thrust through him and a nail in his brain. He makes the serious mistake of stumbling into the center region of the five-pointed star he has drawn with his wife's blood, and there something truly awful happens. In a sickeningly wet sound, his clothes and flesh are simultaneously ripped from his body. For a moment he is a carved cadaver risen from an autopsy table. Then invisible claws go around his head, and he is pulled down and backward, into a pit of nothingness. He just vanishes and I am so grateful that I fall to my knees and weep for a long time.

The spear and nail remain where they have fallen from his body. They lie in the center of the circle. And I know the power of the circle has been broken.

Eventually I climb down the cliff, and walk toward the ocean. I swim away from the hordes of Moslems, who only stare at me as I step onto the beach covered with blood from their dead benefactor. Perhaps they are afraid to touch me, I don't know. But they must have heard stories about Landulf's castle.

The place where magic was performed.

I swim through the waves beyond the invading army.

Beyond reason. The water is clean and stretches forever.

Yet I feel as if I will never be clean again.

16 ～～

When I reach the clear pool of water that same evening, Dante is not there. His absence hits me like a wall. It was too much to hope, I know. But as I sit exhausted beside the pond and stare at the reflection of the vanishing sunlight and the slow emergence of the stars, I ponder the unfairness of life. Here was Dante, a simple man who would give his life for a just cause, killed out of love for me. And here am I, a monster, who will easily kill, and I am still alive. God had granted me a miracle that very morning, yet I feel I would trade all of his grace just to see my friend for a few minutes.

But the night grows darker and still Dante does not come.

He is dead, I know. Death is all I know.

There is blood on my left hand.

The hand that stole the girl's life.

Funny I hadn't noticed it before. Leaning over the pond, I place my hand in the water and try to wash off the dark red stain.

But it does not come off. I wonder why.

"Good. You have passed the first step of initiation. The second step will come later, and then the final and third step."

Killing the girl had been the second step.

Or so he said. That Prince of Lies.

He is dead now. He will say no more.

Not to me. There will be no third initiation.

I scrub my hand fiercely. To no avail.

I have never seen a stain like this before.

"But I am sorry for what I did," I tell the starry pond. "You know I had to do it. I had no choice."

If I am explaining to God, he does not answer me.

But once more my memory of the future is clear. Perhaps the pond acts as a catalyst. It is every bit as clear and round as the one Alanda led me to. And as I could at that watery oasis, I imagine that I can see more reflected stars than I can in the sky itself. My sudden grip on reality makes me marvel at how much my memory faltered while I was embarked on my dark adventure. Maybe Landulf had been blocking me. Maybe my deep-seated fears distorted my memory. I could have tricked myself into not knowing the horrors that awaited me. Or perhaps it was all a function of coming back in time.

I feel as if all my powers, the ones I left behind in the twentieth century, have returned to me. Come back just when I no longer need them. I am surprised, now that my mission is complete, that my staring at the stars does not bring me back to Alanda and Gaia and their spaceship. But maybe I don't want to leave yet. I promised Dante I would wait for him and I am determined to wait. I don't care how long it takes, long past hope I will sit here. Or, indeed, I even consider the possibility of returning to the castle to see if he has been taken captive once more. I could free him, save him.

But the latter is all bravado.

I will not go back to that castle.

I swore it once before and I swear it again.

The stars, as they are reflected in the pond, move lazily on the faint motion of the water. They are beautiful and I feel as if I can stare at them forever. Yet my mood is not peaceful. There is music in my head and it will not go away. I hear a strident refrain from Richard Wagner's *Parsival*. It is almost as if, staring at the heavens, I look upon a vast stage where Wolfram von Eschenbach's *Parsival* is still being played out. I see the knights striving to fulfill their quest for the Grail, and then, Klingsor, in the background, always out of sight, obstructing their every move with his magic wand, the Spear of Longinus. I wonder if I should have left it in Landulf's body. The sacred stabbed through the sinful. But I had feared to approach the center of the pentagram to retrieve it.

Even when he was dead, I was still afraid of him.

It is a truth I have trouble accepting.

I am afraid even now. The stain bothers me.

How was Klingsor stained? What was his mark?

The play explained it all. If only I could remember.

Something about a certain kind of smoothness.

But I cannot remember. No.

Nor can I understand why Dante was so insistent

that I understand the meaning of the Medusa story. He was such a simple fellow, full of phobias and goodness, but when he spoke of mythology, he spoke with great authority. Almost as if another personality used his mouth and lips. I keep feeling as if Dante had been trying to warn me of a deeper threat. One that could not be seen because the true power of the wizard was that he was able to control one's will. Capable of turning whomever he wished to stone, so that he or she did not move unless the wizard wished it.

Could that be the real meaning of the Medusa tale?

The Gorgon did not merely kill her enemies.

She placed them under complete mind control.

Doubts continue to assail me. Questions that are more like ancient riddles. What about the snakes in the hair of Medusa? What about her fair face? Dante had emphasized that the latter was crucial. And I had laughed and told him it was time to concentrate on what was real. But I of all people should have known that reality was not always what it seemed.

A profound certainty sweeps over me.

Dante had been trying to warn me of something *unseen.*

Then I see him. And it is a miracle.

He is struggling up the path to the pond, limping badly, gasping for breath. In a moment I am by his side, helping him to sit down on a large rock not far from the water. He is in worse shape than when I saw him last and is already babbling about how sorry he is that he is late, and why he is late. I can't get a word in, but I am so happy to see him that I weep. Really, it is one of the most wonderful moments of my life. God has heard all of my prayers.

"The passageway was blocked," he says rapidly, with hardly any air in his lungs. "There was a large stone. I had never seen this stone before. Never! My lady, I didn't know what to do. I tried walking back in your direction, but I couldn't find you, and I kept slipping in the water. My brace kept falling off, and once it almost floated away. I would have been crippled! Then I took another path that I know but no one else knows and I went back into the castle and by all the saints in heaven I knew I was going to be put back in the prison. But everyone ignored me! The knights were running all over the place and the servants were crying and it sounded as if something horrible had befallen Lord Landulf." He pauses to breathe and his eyes shine with hope. "What befell him, my lady?" he asks.

I have to smile. Yet there is no joy in it and I wonder why. My happiness is tempered with regrets I can hardly explain to myself.

"He died," I say. "I killed him."

Dante bursts out with laughter. But then he catches himself and quickly does the sign of the cross. But his relief is not to be contained and a moment later he is howling in pleasure again. He jumps up from his rock and hugs me and shakes like a child. Yet the news is too good for him. He is having trouble believing it.

"Is he is really dead?" he keeps asking. "Are you sure it was him? Did you see his body? Are you sure it was his body?"

I strive to calm him. "It was him, I swear it. I put the Spear of Longinus through his evil heart. He died like any other man."

Dante is smiling. "Did you burn his body? Did the smoke stink?"

I shake my head. "No. I didn't burn him. There wasn't time."

His smile falters slightly. "But what did you do with his body, my lady?"

I shrug. "Nothing. I left it. Don't worry, he will not return to haunt us. I am sure of it."

Dante seems reassured. "Then we can go to Messina now and tell everyone that the world is safe?"

I force a laugh. "Yes. We can tell everyone that there is nothing left to worry about." But my laughter soon dies because that is not the way I feel. I add softly, "We will tell the whole world."

Dante is uncertain. "Is something wrong, my lady?"

I turn away. "No. I am just worried about you. You need to eat, to rest and regain your strength."

He stands and steps to my back. "Something weighs on your heart. Share it with me, my lady. Perhaps I can lighten your burden."

My eyes are suddenly damp. I am ashamed to look at his face.

But I feel I can tell him. He will understand.

"When I found Lord Landulf," I say, "he was in the stone circle as you said he would be. But I did not do what you suggested. I did not wait for him to leave the circle to attack him. I was too impatient. He was simply sitting there—I thought I could just kill him and then it would be all over with."

Dante speaks sympathetically. "But you could not penetrate the circle."

My hands clasp each other uneasily. I cannot stop moving them. "Yes. There was an invisible shield around it. Landulf had created it, I believe, by em-

157

ploying a sacrifice that required him to cut out the heart of his own wife."

Dante gasps. "Lady Cia!"

"Yes. She was dead when I arrived. But there was a young woman chained nearby who was very much alive. Landulf told me if I wanted to get to him, I would have to rip out the girl's heart. At first I refused, but then this pounding started in my head, and it wouldn't stop, and I didn't know what to do. In a moment of pain and anger I reached for her . . ." I have trouble finishing. "I reached for her and I—I killed her, Dante. I killed her with my own hands, and she had never done anything to me."

Dante is silent for a long time. Finally I feel his good hand touch my shoulder. "You did what you had to do, my lady."

I clasp his hand but shake my head. "I don't know. Sometimes I think I just did what I have always done in the past—kill. That has always been my ultimate solution to every problem." I gesture weakly. "But this girl—she was praying for me to save her."

"But you saved the rest of us."

I am emotional. "Did I? Did I do what I was supposed to do? If I did then can you explain to me why the stain of this girl's blood refuses to wash off my hand?"

Dante grabs my left hand and stares at it anxiously. "Perhaps we only need to wash it in clean water. Come, my lady, a quick wash in the pond and everything will be all right."

I take back my hand. "No, Dante. I have tried washing it a dozen times. The stain will not come off."

He is confused. "But why?"

I lower my head. "I think it is because I listened to Landulf, in the end."

"No!"

"Yes. I performed the ritual murder of an innocent. That's all that was needed to be initiated by him." I pause and stare at my left hand. There is only the stars for light, but I see the stain well. It is almost as if I see my whole life expressed in the red of the mark. "I have become one of them," I whisper.

Dante is adamant. "No! You are the opposite of them! You are an angel! You bring light where there is darkness! Hope where there is despair! A dozen times you have come to my rescue! A dozen times I would have died without your courage!"

I turn and force a smile. "Oh, Dante. I had to keep saving you because I kept putting you in danger." I raise my hand as he tries to protest. "Please don't look upon me as an angel. When you get to heaven, you'll see real angels and they'll look nothing like me."

He pauses and seems to think hard for a moment. But his eyes never leave my face. "You have too much love in you to be hated by God," he says finally. "When we get to heaven, you'll see that."

I have to laugh and hug him again. "My friend! What would I do without you? No, wait, don't answer that question. There is something I want to do for you. Something I have been planning to do for the last few days. But before I do it I want you to know that it is entirely safe. That no harm will come to your body or soul by the change I am going to bring."

He is curious. "What is this wonderful thing you are going to do?"

I hold his shoulders and stare into his eyes, trying to bring calm and understanding into his excited mind.

"You saw how Landulf was anxious to get my blood? There was a reason for that. Long ago a mysterious man gave me some of his blood, and that blood changed me in a way that made me both strong and resistant to disease. It is impossible for me to get sick. And just a few drops of my blood is able to heal others." I pause. "Do you understand what I am saying, Dante?"

He shakes his head. "I am not sure, my lady."

"I want to cut myself and sprinkle a few drops of my blood over your sores. I know they hurt you terribly, but when a little of my blood touches them they will close and heal. It will be almost be like you never had leprosy. No one will be able to tell by looking at you."

He frowns. "But it is God's will that I am sick. My disease is a punishment for my sins. We cannot change the will of God."

"Your disease is not a punishment. It is not from God. It is something you caught from another person who had the same disease."

He blinks. "From the other lepers in Persida?"

"Exactly. They gave you the leprosy."

He protests. "But I never did anything to them. I only tried to help them."

"But you were around them. You touched them. That is how you got sick."

His confusion deepens. "But Landulf wanted to use your blood, my lady. I should not use it. I should not do anything he wanted to do."

"There is a difference, Dante. Landulf wanted to use my blood to hurt people. I want to use it to heal you."

His superstitions are deep. His disquiet remains.

"But blood should not be shared," he says. "That is what heathens do. When the Holy Father accused my duke, he said that he had been sharing blood with children. I thought at the time that it was lies but it came to pass that it was true. And it was a great evil that Landulf did that. With blood he invoked the demons from hell. The pope saw clearly."

"The pope did not see clearly. Good God, Dante, the pope had you castrated."

His face twitches and his lower lip trembles. I have wounded him with my words and feel ashamed. He drops his head in humiliation.

"I wanted only to do God's will," he moans. "That is all I want to do right now. But I do not know how your blood can make my disease disappear."

I feel I have no recourse. We can argue all night, and get nowhere, and I believe it is possible that he could die this very night. From the burning and the other abuse, his sores are even more inflamed. Half his body is infected tissue, and I feel without even touching him the fever that cooks his blood. The effort it took him to reach me has drained what reserves he had left. His breathing is a perpetual wheeze. If I do not give him my blood soon, I will not be able to return to the future with a clear conscience.

"Dante," I say, meeting his gaze again. "Look at me."

He blinks rapidly. "My lady?"

"Look only at me, my friend. Listen only to me. You do not need to be afraid of my blood. It is a gift from God. Just a few drops of it will make you feel better, and God wants you to feel better after all that you have struggled do in his name."

He is suddenly dreamy. "Yes, my lady."

"Now close your eyes and imagine how nice it will to have your sores healed. How good it will be not to have people run away when they see you because they see you only as a leper. Dante, my dear, I promise you the leprosy will be gone in a few minutes."

"It will be gone," he whispers to himself with his eyes closed.

"Good." I stretch out my hand. "Now keep your eyes closed but give me your hand. I will lead you to the pond and we will first wash your sores and then I will sprinkle something on them and they will be all better."

"All better," he mumbles. But he stiffens when I try to lead him toward the pond even though his eyes remain closed. He is still under my spell, at least I think he is. "No," he says.

I have to speak carefully. "What is the matter?"

"I cannot go in the pond."

"You will not go in the pond, only beside it. I need to wash you off."

"I can drown in the pond," he says.

Now that I think of it, I have never seen Dante wash beside a pond. It is probably one of the reasons he smells.

"I will not let you drown. There is no way you can fall in."

"No," he says.

He appears to be under my spell, but he is resisting me as well. I am reminded of an earlier time when I pressed him for information he knew and yet he managed to evade me—even while in the midst of a powerful hypnotic trance. There is still something in his mind, a psychic aberration of some type, that makes it impossible for me to read him clearly. Even with all my powers now at my disposal, I cannot read what he is thinking exactly.

And I should be able to read his mind completely.

"What if you rest on the rock you were sitting on a moment ago," I suggest. "And I bring you water to clean you. Would that be all right?"

He nods with his eyes closed. "I'll rest on the rock and be all right."

I lead him back to the stone where he initially rested. As he sits, I stroke his head. "I will moisten my shirt," I say. "Then I will touch your sores gently, to clean them. There will be no pain. You will feel nothing but relief. You understand, Dante?"

"I understand," he whispers.

I let go of him. "I will be gone a few seconds. Remain at peace."

He sighs. "Peace."

At the pond the water is very still, more so than ever. Like the pond in the desert, it is a perfect mirror of the heavens. There are so many stars on its delicate surface, so many constellations that it seems almost a sin to disturb the cool liquid. Yet I have stood here before. Last time I also gave Dante my blood and sent him on his way healed of his horrible disease. Like now, and then, I felt moved by love to give him what I could. Certainly he has earned my blood and my trust.

I bend to dampen my shirt and then pause.

I cannot stop staring in the water at the sky. There is the familiar constellation, Andromeda, and I can't remember it ever looking so clear. Why, I can almost imagine that I see Perseus' wife, chained to the rocks as the Titan slowly approaches, bound as a human sacrifice to appease an evil monster. Much as Landulf chained and sacrificed young women to appease his own wickedness. It is incredible, as I look closer, to see Perseus creeping closer to her side, to rescue her, with the Medusa's head hidden in his bag, out of sight. He will only show it at the last moment, when the Titan has exposed himself. Perseus was wise to keep his weapon hidden. It was Dante who suggested that Perseus would have been a fool to part with such power.

Medusa. Perseus. Dante.

"My lady," Dante whispers at my back.

"Coming," I say.

I kneel to wet my shirt.

But once again I pause.

Richard Wagner's opera returns to me on the silence of the night air. The music echoes in my mind with rhythms older than man. Again it is as if I am watching the opera, *Parsival,* being staged against the majestic background of the constellations. Each of the principal characters could be a mythological being. King Arthur could be King Polydectes, who sent Perseus after the Gorgon. Parsival could be Perseus, who slew the Medusa. But who would Klingsor be? Why, of course, the Medusa itself. The one who appears fair from the outside, but whose hair—whose *aura*—is filled with hissing snakes. I understand in that moment that the serpents are symbolically placed above the Medusa's head. They are there so her true identity cannot be mistaken.

"Hurry, my lady," Dante whispers.

I will," I say. But I cannot move, or breathe.

Klingsor and the Medusa. Klingsor and Landulf. They had so much in common.

Except for one little thing. The play spoke of this "thing."

Wolfram von Eschenbach's *Parsival* told of this "thing."

Klingsor had a special mark.

He was smooth—in a delicate spot.

I remember now. Everything.

And I am sick because the truth is horrible beyond belief.

I am turned to stone. Tears cannot help me. They will not come. Not before a pain beyond all measure comes. Because even though I know the truth, I refuse to accept it. My faith may be stronger than stone, but in time all stones are worn away by water. Or tears— it doesn't matter. All I can do now is force my stone body to face what waits behind me.

Wetting my shirt, I stand and spy a lizard that slithers near the side of the pond. In a moment he is in my hand, in my pocket, and I casually walk back to Dante, who sits expectantly on the rock where I left him. A smile springs to his face as I approach even though his eyes remain closed. Leaning over, I begin to gently wipe at his burnt and diseased hand and arm. My touch pleases him.

"Oh, my lady," he says.

"Just relax, Dante," I say softly, "I have to clean you and then I can cure you. You want me to cure you, don't you?"

"Oh, yes."

"Good." I momentarily close my own eyes and bite my lower lip. "That's good."

Seconds later his hand and arm are clean. I stand and reach for the lizard in my pocket. "Now don't be afraid," I say.

"I am not afraid," he whispers.

Placing the lizard behind my back, I pulverize it in my hands. I crush it so hard all the blood squirts into my palms. Then my hands are over Dante's leper sores, dropping the reptile's blood over his wounds. The lizard was cold-blooded; its blood is not so warm as mine would have been. But Dante doesn't seem to notice and for that small favor I am glad. I cannot take my eyes off his face. I am looking for something there, a faint change of expression as his system soaks up my blood. An expression I have not seen before. An expression of triumph, perhaps, or maybe even arrogance. I need to see such a thing to dispel all my questions.

But what I see is much worse.

As the blood sprinkles over him, his lower lip curls ever so slightly. Curls in an unpleasant manner, and I believe deep in my heart that he is reacting to my great sacrifice with all but disguised contempt. I pull my hands away.

"Open your eyes, Dante," I say.

He opens his eyes and beams. "Am I cured, my lady?"

I grin with false pleasure. "Almost, my friend."

Then I grab him by the collar of his filthy shirt and, before he can react, I drag him to the edge of the pond. The water has not completely settled since I touched it, but it is flat enough to show his reflection. No wonder he did not want to stand next to the pond with me by his side. For in the water, Dante's supposedly ruined and pained expression is extraordinary.

Literally, he is more beautiful than a man should be.

He could almost be a goddess.

I leap back from him and tremble.

"Landulf," I gasp. "It was you. All along, it was you."

The other Landulf was just a puppet. Just a disciple of the real master, Dante. The duke in the castle was just a minion.

Dante was the real power behind the throne.

Dante *was* Landulf.

He stares down at his face for a long time before responding. Perhaps he has not seen his reflection in a while—I don't know. When he finally does speak, his voice is remarkably gentle, not unlike it was before, yet with more power, the confidence of a being that has for a long time been master of his own destiny. He straightens as he speaks, as if his physical disease has no real hold over him. But I am not sure if that is the case. He speaks with authority but there is disappointment in his tone.

"I should have guessed you would return with greater wisdom," he says. "Last time you were easily tricked. But now I am the one who has been fooled." He sighs. "You have grown, Sita, in the last thousand years."

"Because I chose wisdom over compassion?" I ask.

He glances at me. "In a sense. It is easier for humans to pass a test of love than a test that requires wisdom. Because even love often obscures wisdom."

I am bitter. "You do not have the right to speak to me of love."

He has been tricked but he still has the ability to smile. "But I do admire you even if I don't love you," he says. "Admiration is the closest my kind gets to love. It serves us well. I never feel the lack of this love you constantly crave."

"You imply that I need something from you. You're wrong."

"Yet you cherished Dante's love," he says.

"I was merely bewildered on the path. You are lost here at the end."

"Perhaps." He pauses. "How did you guess?"

"Parsival. I saw it in Vienna before World War Two. The character of Klingsor was Landulf. He had been castrated by the pope." I mock him. "In the play, they said he was smooth between the legs."

A wave of anger rolls over his face but he quickly masters himself. "You have an excellent memory. No doubt I made other mistakes with you as well."

"Yes. But I am puzzled. Why did you give me the clue of the Medusa's head?"

"It was necessary. For you to be totally mine, you had to be warned by me in advance. Free will operates on both paths, the right and the left. When you intentionally killed that girl, then and only then were you made ready to meet me here."

"It was all just a set up? The whole thing?"

"Yes."

"And had I willingly given you my blood, I would have completed the third step?"

"Precisely. Then your blood would have been of the most use to me."

I sigh. "Well, I guess now you're not going to have it."

He stares at me. I see him clearly now, his supernatural beauty, even the faint tendrils of black that crawl around the field above his head. Yet I realize he still has leprosy.

"You are wrong on that point," he says softly.

I take a step back. "You are still about to die. You need my blood to live even a few more days. Your evil invocations really did give you leprosy.

He takes a step in my direction. "That is correct. The work has its price. But I need your blood to sustain this physical body, and continue my work in this third density. But unlike last time, I will now be unable to pass my blood onto others. You can no longer be convinced to be my initiate and undergo a shift toward negative polarization. Still, your blood will be useful to me for a long time." He removes a dagger from under his dirty shirt. It is the same one that the maid stabbed me with. It is stained with my blood. "There is no point in trying to run from me, Sita, or in trying to harm me. My psychic powers are beyond yours."

I find it impossible to turn away from him.

Indeed, I cannot even move my arms or legs

The Medusa. My body has turned to stone.

"It doesn't matter what you do to me now," I say, thankful to be able to use my tongue. "I have defeated you and the rest of your kind. In the future there will be no army of invincible negative beings to confuse humanity. Your cancer has been cut from society. The harvest will go forward the way it was intended. You have lost, Landulf, admit it."

He steps to within two feet of me. He brushes my long hair with his knife. Then he licks the tip of the blade, the dried blood, and smiles sadly.

"It is not my nature to admit anything," he says. "But I will say that I would have enjoyed your continuing adoration almost as much as your body, and the immortal blood that pumps through it." He scratches the skin below my right eye and a red drop runs over my cheek. The sight fills him with pleasure. "A vampiric tear, Sita. Cried for me? I must still be your hero."

I am defiant, and no longer afraid.

The stain on my left hand has vanished.

"My only regret is the tears I cried for you," I say. "Other than that I have none. I am at peace. And you are still a monster. One day you will be forced to look in Perseus' mirror, and you will see your own reflection, and see just how foul you are to behold. And on that day you will turn to stone, Landulf. You will die and rot, and the world will be relieved of a great burden." I stop. "Kill me now and get it over with. If you have the nerve, you disgusting creature!"

I spit in his face. He does not like that.

He wipes the saliva away and raises his knife.

"I was going to kill you quick," he says. "But now, Sita, it may take all night."

He moves to slit open my side and then pauses, puzzled.

I am confused as well, for a moment. My body has begun to glow. The pond shines as well, with the light of the heavens. It is as if the constellations in the sky have been awakened, and been inspired to send down their light to Earth. The white light that fills my body comes from the direction of the pond as well as the sky. Landulf seems to recognize the transformation I am undergoing and is filled with dismay. But this stellar current fills me with euphoria. I have experienced it before, just before I rescued the child from the Setians. Landulf is like one of those creatures, I see, only worse. He struggles to cut into my flesh as I grow brighter. His frustration makes me laugh.

"I guess you're going to have to remain a leper," I say in a voice that grows faint. "But don't take it too hard. You're not going to be around much longer. Yaksha is still somewhere on this planet and you might try to find him, but I don't think that you'll get to him in time. As far as you're concerned, I am the last vampire. Your last chance, Landulf. How does that feel?"

His rage is incredible to behold. The fair face of the god is transformed into a demon. The all but invisible serpents above his head hiss poisonous vapors. They surround him in a noxious cloud. It is as if his whole body has been swallowed by his leper's sores. He tries to grab me but his fingers pass through me. Seeing his efforts are useless, he strains to regain his pleasant demeanor, to make one last stab at my soul. But he still has the knife in his hand and in either case I will never be fooled by him again.

"Sita," he says. "Our offer is still good. We can grant you powers unimaginable. You have only to join us, and we will rule this world together."

I am practically a ghost but I can still laugh.

"You shouldn't have mentioned the togetherness part," I reply. "I can't think of anything more dull."

17 ~~~

There is a brief moment when I am lying on the floor of the interstellar craft. I feel Alanda and Gaia close. It is possible Alanda even calls my name. She must know I have successfully completed my mission. She must be waiting for me, to smile at me, to take me to other worlds, into a glorious future.

But my battle with Landulf has taken something from me.

Finally I am tired of such adventures.

As Yaksha finally grew weary, I also crave a change.

Before Alanda can call me back to the present moment, I focus my entire being on another page of history. I return to the first vampire, the strange night Yaksha was born, five thousand years ago in India, when I was a girl of seven years. The Aghoran ceremony has ended and the evil priest has been killed by Amba's animated corpse. The corpse finally lies down but there is movement inside Amba's belly, which is still swollen with the nine-month-old fetus she was carrying when she died. My father takes his knife and goes to cut out the unborn child trapped in the womb. I leap from my hiding place behind the bushes.

"Father!" I cry, as I reach for his hand that holds the knife. "Do not let that child come into the world. Amba is dead, see with your own eyes. Her child must likewise be dead. Please, Father, listen to me."

Naturally, all the men are surprised to see me, never mind hear what I have to say. My father is angry with me, but he kneels and speaks to me patiently.

"Sita," he says, "your friend does appear dead, and we were wrong to let this priest use her body in this way. But he has paid for his evil karma with his own life. But we would be creating evil karma of our own if we do not try to save the life of this child. You remember when Sashi was born, how her mother died before she came into the world? It sometimes happens that a living child is born to a dead woman."

"No," I protest. "That was different. Sashi was born just as his mother died. Amba has been dead since early dawn. Nothing living can come out of her."

My father gestures with his knife to the squirming life inside Amba's bloody abdomen. "Then how do you explain the life here?"

"That is the yashini moving inside her," I say. "You saw how the demon smiled at us before it departed. It intends to trick us. It is not gone. It has entered into the child."

173

My father ponders my words with a grave expression. He knows I am intelligent for my age, and occasionally asks my advice. He looks to the other men for guidance, but they are evenly divided. Some want to use the knife to stab the life moving inside Amba. Others are afraid, like my father, of committing a sin. Finally my father turns back to me and hands me the knife.

"You knew Amba better than any of us," he says. "You would best know if this life that moves inside her is evil or good. If you know for sure in your heart that it is evil, then strike it dead. None of the men here will blame you for the act."

I am appalled. I am still a child and my father is asking me to commit an atrocious act. But my father is wiser than I have taken him for. He shakes his head as I stare at him in amazement, and he moves to take back the knife.

But I don't give the knife to him.
I know in my heart what I must do.
I stab the blade deep into Amba's baby.
Black blood gushes over my hands.
But it is only the blood of one. Not thousands.
The creature inside Amba's body stops moving.

Alanda turns to Gaia after studying her friend's body. They are not in a spaceship, but stand in the desert at night beside a clear pond. Many stars shine overhead.

"She is not breathing," Alanda says. "Her heart has stopped."

"But she stopped him," Gaia says, who actually can

speak in his own way. "The path is now clear for many."

Alanda glances down at her friend. There is sorrow in her voice. "But she was coming back to us," she says.

Gaia comforts her. "She always went her own path. Let her go this way."

Yet Alanda later sheds a tear as they slide her friend's body into the pond. For a moment her friend floats on the surface of the water, and the reflection of the stars frame her figure. And when Alanda glances up, she sees the same outline in the heavens. For a moment her friend is constellation and it gives her a measure of comfort. But when Alanda looks back down, her friend has sunk beneath the mirror of the water and is gone.

"It is like she never was," Alanda whispers.

"It is like that for all of us," Gaia says.

One moonless night, when I am twenty years of age, I am awakened by a sound outside. Besides me sleeps my husband, Rama, and on my other side is our daughter, Lalita. I don't know why the sound wakes me. It was not loud. But it was peculiar, the sound of nails scraping over a blade. I get up and go outside my house and stand in the dark and look around.

For a long time I stand there, expecting to meet someone.

But there is no one there.

Finally I return to my bed and fall asleep.

The next morning I am playing with my Lalita by the river when a strange man comes by. He is tall and powerfully built. In his right hand he holds a lotus flower, in his left a gold flute. His legs are long and his every movement is bewitching. I cannot help but stare at him, and I am delighted when he comes and kneels beside me on the bank of the river. For some reason, I know he means me no harm.

"Hello," he says, staring at the water. "How are you?"

"I am fine." I pause. "Do I know you, sir?"

A faint smile touches his lips. "Yes. We have met before."

I hesitate. He does seem familiar but I cannot place him.

"I am sorry, I don't remember," I say.

He finally looks at me and his eyes are very blue. They remind me of the stars at night; they seem to sparkle with light from the heavens. "My name is Krishna," he says.

I bow my head. "I am Sita. This is my daughter, Lalita. Are you new to this area?"

He turns back to the water. "I have been here before."

"Is there anything I can do for you? Would you like some food?"

He glances at me, out the corners of his eyes, and I feel a thrill in my heart. There is such love in his glance, I don't understand how it can be so. "I was wondering if I could do anything for you, Sita," he says.

"My Lord?" I ask, and I feel he is deserving of the title.

He shrugs faintly. "I merely came to see if you were happy. If you are, then I will be on my way."

I have to laugh. "My Lord, I am not long married. My husband is a wonderful man whom I love dearly and God has seen fit to grace us with a beautiful child. We are all healthy and have plenty to eat. I cannot imagine being any happier than I am right now."

He nods briefly and then stands. "Then I will say goodbye, Sita."

But I jump up. "You came all the way here just to see if I was happy?"

"Yes." His eyes are kind as he looks at me for the last time. "Your happiness is all that matters to me. Remember me, Sita."

Then he walks away and I never see him again.

But I never forget him. Krishna.

Epilogue ～

Seymour Dorsten sat at his computer in his bedroom and stared at the words on the screen. It was late, close to dawn, and he had been writing most of the night. For the last six months, in fact, he had worked almost every night without rest. But it didn't matter how much sleep he missed. He could always sleep during the day. Because he was very sick with AIDS, he no longer attended school, or even went out of the house. Indeed, his personal physician thought he wouldn't live out the year, and it was almost Christmas. Yet the tragedy of his early demise did not disturb him, at least not at the moment. Like his imagined heroine, he was happy in the end, to have even reached the end.

He had just finished his story. *Her* story.

About Alisa Perne, his Sita. The Last Vampire.

Seymour felt as if he had taken her everywhere she could go, but at the same time he knew that it was *she* who had led him on the adventures. Lifted him up to heights he could not have imagined if not for his serious illness. For him, the constant experience of his waning mortality had been the greatest muse. She had never said who she was sending her thoughts out to, but it was to him, always to him. But *he* had made her immortal, and himself, so that he wouldn't have to be afraid of his own death. He knew, in the end, that she had not been afraid, and that her only regret had been that she had not been able to say goodbye to him. But at least he could say goodbye to her.

Seymour leaned forward and turned off the screen.

There was a noise outside his window.

He glanced over. Quickly, he always did.

But it was nothing. A cat, the wind.

But such sounds, this late at night, always made him think of her. Ageless Sita coming through the window to give him her magical blood. To save him from his illness. But she had chosen the only destiny worthy of her. She had simply decided to vanish, to exist only in his heart.

Seymour coughed weakly and brushed away a tear that came to his eye. He should be in a hospital. His lungs were half-filled with fluid, and he couldn't draw in a full breath without pain. Still, he thought, it was better to be at home with his computer and his story. He just wished his heart could beat for her forever.

Seymour was going to miss her. Yeah.
"Goodbye, Sita," he said to the empty screen.
He thought he would miss her forever.

THE END

Look for Christopher Pike's

EXECUTION OF INNOCENCE

and

THE TACHYON WEB

Coming mid-November 1996

About the Author

CHRISTOPHER PIKE was born in Brooklyn, New York, but grew up in Los Angeles, where he lives to this day. Prior to becoming a writer, he worked in a factory, painted houses, and programmed computers. His hobbies include astronomy, meditating, running, playing with his nieces and nephews, and making sure his books are prominently displayed in local bookstores. He is the author of *Last Act, Spellbound, Gimme a Kiss, Remember Me, Scavenger Hunt, Final Friends* 1, 2, and 3, *Fall into Darkness, See You Later, Witch, Die Softly, Bury Me Deep, Whisper of Death, Chain Letter 2: The Ancient Evil, Master of Murder, Monster, Road to Nowhere, The Eternal Enemy, The Immortal, The Wicked Heart, The Midnight Club, The Last Vampire, The Last Vampire 2: Black Blood, The Last Vampire 3: Red Dice, Remember Me 2: The Return, Remember Me 3: The Last Story, The Lost Mind, The Visitor, The Last Vampire 4: Phantom* and *The Last Vampire 5: Evil Thrist*, all available from Archway Paperbacks. *Slumber Party, Weekend, Chain Letter,* and *Sati*—an adult novel about a very unusual lady—are also by Mr. Pike.